FIRST DOG ON EARTH

IRV WEINBERG

FIRST DOG ON EARTH
A NOVEL BY IRV WEINBERG

ISBN 979-8-7840-5700-6

Direction by Irv Weinberg with Suzanne Leonard
Authored by Irv Weinberg
Editing by Sagacity Publishing Group
Production by Audivita Studios

Cover design by Steve Wedeen
Book design by Cassidy Reynolds, Weeva, Inc.
Illustrations by Molly Dwight, Weeva, Inc.

Published by Sagacity Publishing Group
Printed and Distributed by Weeva, Inc.

First printed in the United States of America
First Printing, 2020

Visit FirstDogBook.com

FIRST DOG

ON EARTH

AN ORIGINAL STORY, BEAUTIFULLY TOLD

"As I write this review, my dog Peaches sits by my side, her warm furry body resting on my foot. I feel the loyalty, I embrace the love. But where did this extraordinary man/dog connection come from? In this highly original novel, Irv Weinberg takes us back to the primal beginnings when a wolf and a man first conquered fear, tribal jealousy and a cold angry world - and learned to trust, protect, and love one another. The story is fresh, original and a great read."

—HOWIE COHEN
AUTHOR, ADVERTISING CREATIVE DIRECTOR, CLIO HALL OF FAME

"I was intrigued by a story of the First Dog on Earth, a topic I'd never even considered before. The author created a tale that was not only captivating, but very mind provoking. Where DID humans learn so much of what we take for granted including our relationship with canines? This book is one of the best I've ever read and I highly recommend it."

—THOMAS RAVEY
CEO HABITAT VERDE

"Irv (no last name needed), an author who weaves fiction into nonfiction like Dali blends the surreal into reality. First Dog On Earth is so much more than a book, it is a story of biblical significance. It is the story of hope, love and humanity through the interrelationships of dog and man."

—MICHAEL SMITH
CEO INDEPENDENCE LIGHTING CORP

"I knew Irv Weinberg in the advertising business. He was known for his quick wit and brilliant use of words that so often had a sort of shock value alongside his humor! He created a legend of himself and now I am compelled to say he has written a legendary book. First Dog will not be the last we hear of Irv Weinberg. Of that I am certain."

—ELISABETH NOONE
VOICE OVER/ON CAMERA ACTOR

A book about love for the man who taught me
its meaning, my grandfather, Meyer Weinberg

PREFACE

In the spring of 1994, a team of cave explorers stumbled into the find of a lifetime. A treasure trove of prehistoric art painted onto the walls of Chauvet Cave in Southern France. These now famous paintings, dating back more than 30,000 years, are considered to be among the world's greatest works of art.

But just as astonishing as the art on the walls was what they found on the cave's floor. A fossilized trail of footprints, left behind by a small boy and his dog that stretched on for more than 150 feet.

The relaxed shapes of their footprints tell a story of the trust, care and affection these two must have shared as they walked calmly together into the darkness of the cave.

The companionship and love between humans and dogs. It's a tale as old as time. A tale every person who has ever had the privilege to love and be loved by a dog can understand. This is the story of that first dog that consciously left the company of wolves and joined the family of man.

SECTION

HOW IT ALL BEGAN

1

CHAPTER 1

The she-wolf dragged her swollen belly across the rough dirt floor to a cool, quiet corner at the back of the den. Enough moons had passed and now the time had come.

Panting hard, she pushed back at the pain and pushed out the first of her five pups that entered the world wet and bloody, not knowing how much they had changed it.

One by one she licked them clean and nudged them to her waiting nipples. She watched them tumble and fumble over each other until they learned to hang on and feed. Born hungry, they learned quickly.

The she-wolf ran her nose over each of them, drawing in their essence, drawing in their scents and locking them in her memory. This was not her first litter. She had seen many others being born, as all in the pack had, but never one like this one.

A bolt of cold fear ran across her spine as she felt the warmth of their tiny bodies against her. In the wolf pack, differences were dangerous things. They made you an outsider and being an outsider made you prey.

Month after month the she-wolf kept her quickly growing puppies apart from the rest of the pack, hoping that given time they would change enough to blend in. But the differences grew more obvious.

Their bodies stayed smaller and sleeker. Their eyes looked larger and closer together. Their behavior was more trusting and tamer, more curious and playful, more approachable and affectionate. And they were smarter by far than any of the other pups around them.

Before the sun began to climb, the she-wolf knew the day had come. Her pups' differences could no longer go unnoticed.

She would not let the old alpha male or any of the other males of the pack vying for leadership prove their virility with the blood of her pups.

In the dim light of early morning while the rest of the pack was still asleep, she nudged her pups awake and led them farther into the forest than they had ever been before and turned her back on them.

They would either live or die, according to the will of nature and the moods of the gods. Better that, the she-wolf knew, than in the jaws of the old alpha or any of the hungry pack.

At first the pups, always at her side, did not understand as she pushed them off and backed away. But each time they tried to come close to her, she snarled and lunged at them until they turned and ran away, their tails wrapped tightly beneath them.

The gods took pity as the fleeing pack followed Oohma, as he would one day be called, south, always south toward the warming sun. They were not alone. The earth was on the move again as the returning sun began to warm the planet.

Each day as night ended, Oohma looked up at the black ribbons of birds unspooling across the sky. Oohma knew birds know what others don't. Not just what is in the sky around them but on the earth below them. Where they flew Oohma and the pack would follow.

As they traveled south, the land of cold they had come from faded from their memories. The weather now was more agreeable, food more plentiful, shelter easier to find. Nothing unknown or dangerous had come at them from the thick brush and forest all around them. Not yet.

CHAPTER 2

The moment the beating of wings shattered the stillness of the air, Oohma brought the pack to their feet with a booming howl. They locked their eyes on Oohma, shaking their bodies into a high state of readiness, ready to follow where he led.

Racing for the light, he flew down the rocky crag into the open air. The cool, soft earth felt good under his sore pads, making his tail wag. If the days ahead were like the days that passed, there would be a lot of ground to cover and a lot of running to do.

The pack's sharp eyes swept the earth as they ran, taking in everything around them. The tender green shoots that poked through the softening ground. The branches of trees, heavy with nuts and fruit. Grasses bent from the weight of their seeds at their heads.

On the hillsides herds grazed on the new, young growth. In the rivers low swooping flies made fish fat. And everywhere on the rich dark soil hundreds of small creatures, grown lazy from nature's bounty, made easy prey. Even for the young and inexperienced pack.

They stopped only once during the day to rest and water and again as darkness neared, to hunt and eat and sleep. Their pace was easy. Their steps relaxed. Nothing escaped their sharp senses, even those they couldn't see.

The winds that had been gentle turned suddenly from the east, rattling the trees' branches and ruffling the pack's fur. They felt it surround them and it pushed them close together.

Raising their heads they pulled at the wind as hard as Oohma did and the hair on their necks stood up just as straight. The smell the forest fears more than any other was rushing up at them. The smell of smoke.

The pack was ready to turn and run. Oohma did not let them. The smoke was there but it was not everywhere, just in one tight spot, not spreading and roaring. Still they could not ignore it. A fire dying or one coming alive, young and hungry, could be the difference between life and death.

Moving fast they closed in as night fell. And there it was again. But this time they sensed more than smoke. Something was with it. Something they had never known before. And that was not a good thing. Not knowing what was coming never ends well.

Oohma circled nervously and snapped at the air. The low growl rattling out of him was echoed by the pack. Now that he had it, he took it in and rolled it over again and again to learn its secrets.

It was sharp and acrid like a dead thing that had yet to be taken by the ground. But dead things were not new to the pack. This was not that, but something else.

The more the new scent surrounded him, the deeper he drew it in, the more his head rocked back and forth. But still he could not understand it or what it might be. How could something be more than what it is? And why did that thing keep changing?

Sometimes it was mixed with bear. Sometimes fox and lion or roebuck, rabbit or squirrel or other beasts the pack knew well. And there was not one of them but a pack of them, moving at them, through the trees.

Oohma stood rock still. Only his head moved as the scents kept moving at him, getting stronger as they did. But still they did not tell him the thing the pack needed to know. How could one thing be more than the thing it was? And if it were, how much more dangerous would that make it?

CHAPTER 3

All day the band of hunters, their rangy, slinking bodies covered by crudely sewn skins trailed the birds heading north. The sun, hot on their backs, had been without mercy since their trek began, exhausting them of energy and food and spirit.

Still they moved on each day until the sun dropped from the sky and the birds could no longer be seen against the growing darkness.

The threat behind them had grown greater each day as the precious rain and storm and thunder became a distant memory. All around them green things became dead things and every animal became a competitor for the same few plants and prey. Not knowing where, the tribe trudged on. Better to suffer searching for food than to stay behind and starve.

Hun, their leader, a brutish man of 25, with arms like thick vines and legs like tree stumps, raised his hand and all stopped to rest, dropping their spears and small sacks beneath a rocky overhang.

Putting their exhaustion aside, the males spread out to gather up firewood while the females piled handfuls of dried grasses inside a quickly drawn circle of stone.

When the wood was placed on top of the grasses, Hun drew two blocks of black flint out of a leather sack and struck them against each other until an orange spark jumped into the dried grasses. Bending low he blew the glow into life and a wispy puff of smoke grew into a flame.

Once the fire was going, a crude campsite began to grow around it. The females of the tribe spread out to gather nuts and berries to stretch the meat, still fresh enough to eat, into their evening meal. That would keep them going but only for a while.

Twenty-four of them had started north. Twenty-two now survived. Two of the hunters had been killed along the way by a pair of forest lions as they stalked a deer bending its head to eat the grasses in a clearing.

The deer's eyes were on the grass not the hunters and the hunter's ears were on the deer not the lions moving up behind them. The roar spun them around, just in time to see the last moment of their lives.

All that was left when the lions were finally driven off were the torn arm of one and the chewed-up torso of the other. These were laid on the ground and covered with flowers, rocks and twigs.

Two other tribesmen were injured in a hopeless attempt to save their companions. They took deep slashes but survived because of the old female who had been taught the healing arts by her own grandmother, the medicine woman of the tribe.

CHAPTER 4

Nuun was her name. Ancient at 52, born before any of the others could remember, in the times the legends talked about. Her face, shrunken and shriveled, was etched by age. So were her breasts, sucked dry by the countless children she had given birth to, mostly dead before their second year of life.

Once, Nuun's eyes were clear and bright and she could see to the horizon and deep into the valleys. Now she could barely see her own hand. Each day, the white clouds that floated on her dark brown eyes grew thicker and denser. But she had yet to find a plant that could drive them away.

Years of softening hides and fibrous roots had ground her teeth to dull, black nubs, making it hard to chew. But what was still sharp was her mind. The knowledge of what she had been taught stayed with her and grew in her, even as her strength began to die.

Nuun knew the yellow yarrow, with its wide, spiky heads, could be dried and mixed with plantain to stop wounds from bleeding. Goldenrods could be chewed and swallowed to heal deep inside. Wild lettuce could stop pain. The sweet scent of lavender could keep stinging insects at bay. And the buds of the spiked plant she gathered and dried could make them speak to their ancestors and see visions in the night.

None of the tribe received food they did not hunt for or gather. Even nursing mothers had to hold their babies in one arm while taking food with the other. But Nuun was like no other. The medicine woman's magic set her apart.

It came with a heavy price. All that was known by the tribe was known by Nuun. If that knowledge were lost, there would be no tribe.

Nuun had a granddaughter, a dull young girl called Lut, with a nest of black hair, dark eyes and breasts just beginning to bud. She roamed the vast forest on her strong young legs to find the plants and roots Nuun needed.

Nuun's own legs had grown too old and bent to take her much farther than a pit beyond the fire to relieve herself. So she accepted Lut's ignorance in exchange for her endurance.

She had no choice, but she could not conceal her concern or contempt. Over and over she had shown the girl the needed plants and how to prepare them, their seasons and their uses and how to dry and blend them with other plants when needed.

At first Nuun did it slowly, but her patience was as thin as her body and her anger over Lut's mistakes often got the better of her. When it did, it drove her up on her weakened legs, to slap and punch the dull girl's face.

All the tribe's legends and knowledge were in Nuun's hands and all she had to hand them to was a granddaughter she did not trust. But there was nothing else she could do. Healing was women's work and all her other grandchildren were males.

CHAPTER 5

Lut left before the sun had risen and before the fires were lit. She kept the pictures of what Nuun needed behind her eyes while her feet pounded the ground.

The injured hunters needed attention if they were ever to heal. Only, the plants Nuun needed to save them were in the fields and the forest, not in her medicine bag.

A well-worn path stretched out in front of her, but off to the side an over-grown game trail she hadn't noticed before caught her eye. She turned, caught her breath and pushed her way along it.

The thick underbrush snapped at her, slapping her arms and face. Thick clouds of insects swarmed around her, darting in for her sweat and her blood. Still, she did not stop. The hunters' pain was greater.

With the growing light came the rising heat, making her breath come hard and her tongue stick to the roof of her mouth. She had to stop. She could not help it. She could go without food but not without water.

Between her panting breaths she heard the trickle of a small stream just below the grassy hill. Pulling her tongue over her dry, cracked lips she swallowed hard and walked down to it.

She crabbed across the slippery rocks and found a fallen tree at the edge of the stream. Reaching down for it, she steadied herself as best she could, bent her knees and drank until she could drink no more and splashed her forehead and neck with the cool, clear water.

The rotting log lay over a grayish white circle. Nuun had taught Lut some mushrooms healed but others caused violent, painful death. These seemed too narrow and delicate to be dangerous and hours had passed since she had eaten. And there they were, at her feet.

She stretched her neck and laid her head on the cool, damp ground, pressing her nose against the earthy blooms. There was little to sense but wet and dirt. Pulling one up by its stem she shook it clean, hesitated for a second and put it in her mouth.

The taste was mild and pleasant, almost sweet. Once she had eaten one she wanted more and her hunger grew with each swallow. In minutes the circle between her knees disappeared as she took the last one and washed it down with another handful of cool water.

At first there was nothing, just the feeling of having eaten, just the feeling of feeling full. But then a humming flew up from deep inside her, like a nest of yellow jackets she had tripped over with her foot.

The sound did not stay inside her but jumped out of her mouth and filled the valley. A strong gust of wind rushed up at her, lifting her into the air above the forest. Spreading her arms out as far as they would go, she glided through the canopy of trees and floated back to earth.

The sound of thunder spun her around when she landed, but there was none to hear, just her pounding heart. She needed to reach back for something she knew, or how would she find her way back again?

She forced herself to breathe. To fix her eyes on something solid, to make her grandmother's words come back to her. Yarrow yes, yarrow, the leaves that stopped bleeding, those she could remember, but the rest? She could not summon their look or their names.

She slapped at her head again and again, but they would not come to her, just flashes of color and shafts of light that surrounded her with every blow.

Soon the thunder softened along with her vision. The colors of the landscape became separate again, but she saw them as never before, vivid and shimmering and alive.

Off in a close-by meadow, made by an age-old fire, a carpet of intense green with tall stalks of yellow sticking out of it came into view. Swaying back and forth, the yellow yarrows waved to her.

She fell back in terror when she heard them call her name. "Lut, Lut," they said. "Don't be afraid. We are here, the ones that stop bleeding." Another pulled her head down. It was the wild lettuce whispering from below, "I am here, the one that stops pain." Farther off in the green fields, the grasses swayed and sang to her as one. "Come take us, we will teach you what to do."

The branch of a tree beckoned to her at the edge of the clearing. When she stood beneath it, a lush yellow mango brushed against her hand. She heard its sweet voice say, "Taste us, you will see."

She reached out and took a ripe one. Its luscious juices flowed down her chin when she bit into it.

Never had she tasted sweetness like that before. How would she ever describe the taste, even to herself, when there were no words yet for what she did not know?

CHAPTER 6

She raced to the field as fast as her legs would carry her. Bending down, reaching out, she gathered and plucked and slashed with her blade until her basket was filled with all her grandmother needed and more. Things even with all her wisdom and all her years, Nuun had never known.

Lut grunted softly to herself and the hint of an upturn crossed her tight lips. Had she made a mistake again and returned with the wrong plants or none at all, it could mean the lives of the wounded hunters and perhaps her own life as well. Nuun was old and her limbs were withered, but when she had to, she could blacken an eye or loosen a tooth.

But Lut had secrets now. Ones the trees and the earth had whispered to her. Ones they shared with few. What they had told her was beyond treasure. Beyond anything her grandmother had ever known. They had made Lut their sister.

There was something else they whispered to her as she raced back toward the camp. Not her grandmother or anyone else, especially Hun, would raise a hand to her or touch her. Not ever.

With her heart and her basket full, Lut returned to the campsite, an unusual glow surrounding her face. She ducked her head under the leather skin to the place her grandmother sat waiting, pulling a strip of vine through a sheet of hide with a sharp, thin bone.

Lut didn't make a sound but lifted the basket high above her head. Spinning in a circle, she dumped it at Nuun's feet. Nuun's old eyes bulged as she ran her hand over all Lut had brought her. There was more than she asked for. More than she had ever seen. More than she had ever known.

Nuun took some to her nose and put some in her mouth. When she had tasted what Lut had gathered, the clouds on her dim eyes parted and Lut was there before her, shimmering with light.

She crawled over and touched Lut's ears and knew she had heard them. She touched her head and knew it had been told to her. Nuun shook hers back and forth and a chuckle cracked open her dry old lips.

After a moment, Nuun reached for the petals of yarrow and turned them into a paste. Then she turned and made her way to the hunters still groaning in pain from the lion's claws. Both had mercifully fallen into a swoon, unable to endure the pain or the raging fever that fired through their bodies.

Once the paste had stopped the blood seeping from their wounds, Nuun motioned for the girl to bring her medicine bag. A sack of softened leather made from the udder of a forest cow, cinched at the top with a leather cord.

From the sack Nuun pulled out a bone with a hole punched into its end, sharper and thinner than the one she used to sew her hides. She forced a strand of thin sinew through the hole at its top and pulled it taut. A few swift stitches closed the wound of one hunter before she turned to the other.

With the wounds stitched, she took the wild lettuce leaves the girl had foraged and crushed them with the tool her son had made for her before he died. She mixed this with a few drops of water that she dripped into each of the hunters' mouths. In a few moments she could see the plants' effect as the bodies relaxed and they slept even deeper.

When Nuun had finished with the wounded hunters, she turned her face to Lut again. Even her dim eyes could see that Lut's eyes, once dark coals, were now on fire.

Tears filled the deep-set lines on her wrinkled face. A feeling of peace settled over her. The weight on her shoulders lifted as she reached for Lut's hand and took it in hers and brought it to her lips.

Lut looked at her grandmother when she felt it, but Nuun did not look back. A curve crossed Nuun's lips as her head slumped onto her chest and a deep sigh wheezed out of her. Lut was the medicine woman now. Nuun was moving for the clouds.

CHAPTER 7

The pack moved in closer as the unknown scent grew stronger. Oohma stole to the edge of the thicket, where he could see what was coming without being seen.

His hair bristled at the sound they made moving through the forest. How fearsome they must be to move so loudly, when even the most powerful move carefully.

Along with the sounds of their movement came the sounds that went among them. Grunts and clicks and whistles that made no more sense to Oohma than the neighing of a horse. But they seemed to understand each other's clicks by making more.

One loud snap and then another and the brush parted. Oohma's tight mouth fell open as the first of them came into the light.

They had seen animals of all kinds as they traveled south. Some they knew and some they didn't. But no matter how different they all were, there was one thing they all shared. Four legs.

But not the ones stepping out of the brush. They walked on two, their back paws holding them up straight and steady. Something he or the pack could do, but only for a moment.

Oohma took a step back, his eyes never leaving them, a low growl rumbling out of him. The more he saw, the more he knew they were not like anything he had ever seen before.

With their front paws, they could drag and pull things. Even the pack's strong jaws could not lift and carry and walk the way these could.

One of them, a male, used his long front paws to pull up into a tree. He reached out and tore at the fruit. When he had one, he dropped it to another of them who reached out his front paws and caught it before it hit the ground.

When the rising sun took the heat up with it, something else about these animals came to light. Part of them must be snake or how could they reach up and shed their skins? And when they did, they were not different things but only one thing again. What other, anywhere could do that?

Oohma's head cocked back and forth as he watched them. Finally he began to understand. They had their own skins, but they wore the skins of others over theirs. There was no mistaking the meaning of that. Any animal that could rip the skins off a lion or a bear was something powerful and cunning. Something the pack had to know.

As the sky darkened, Oohma saw the leader turn and bark a command. The tribe stopped what they were doing and dropped, exhausted, to the ground. The leader let them rest for a while. Then he spun his hand. The males stood and clicked angry sounds as they bent for stones they placed in a circle.

Now their females jumped in, putting bundles of dried grasses into the circle and stepping back. The one who seemed the leader took two black stones, one in each front paw, then bent down and struck them against each other until a yellow spark flew out.

CHAPTER 8

Oohma was on his paws as he saw him kneel down and blow on the spark until a wisp of smoke, then a lively flame jumped up. Every muscle inside Oohma tensed. But his need to know was far greater than his need to escape. Slowly he crawled back to the edge of his perch.

Fire was the enemy of every animal in the forest, of every branch and every blade of grass and every tree. It meant one thing to all that lived in it. Run away as fast as you can.

But these new ones did not run from it. They ran at it. They drew close to it and poked at it, feeding it wood to keep it alive and glowing into the night.

Oohma's eyes narrowed as he watched them sit close to it. Fire was not their enemy. Fire was their friend and the smoke they smelled came from their flames, not the forests.

For long hours Oohma watched. Pulling them apart with every sense he had. Their rough faces, their harsh smell, listening to the clicks and whistles that went among them. But his eyes crunched down even tighter at what he saw next. Their females took strips of meat and threw them onto the flames.

The pack knew what fire does to meat. Turns it into black lumps no animal, no matter how hungry, would eat. But that did not stop them. They threw in more.

Stabs of wind drove the flames higher, making the meat sizzle on the hot stones. The scent of it hit Oohma's nose like a clap of thunder. Streams of drool hung from his mouth and his paws scratched the dirt.

Never had anything startled him that way. It took all his strength to fight the urge tearing through him. To race out of his lair, to fly at them from the dark and snatch the morsel away.

But his survival instincts returned his reason. Better to stay a while longer, knowing there would be more to see. Knowing there was more to take in, before he made a move.

He saw one of them stand up and reach for a smooth branch with a point of stone. As the others yelped and clicked, he pointed at a tree at the edge of their clearing and pulled his front paw back.

His arm shot forward again, sending the branch flying through the air like an eagle, straight through the thin trunk of the tree. When it hit, all the males hit their branches on the ground and made their clicking sounds.

Oohma and his pack were deadly hunters when they could get in close, after they had chased down and surrounded their exhausted prey. But never could they take one down from 50 feet away. That no animal, no bird, no fish, no snake could do.

CHAPTER 9

All of the tribe sat close to it, their gruff faces made even more gruesome by the flickering light of the flames. The men's jaws were covered with fur, as were parts of their bodies. But the women's fur was only on their heads. Except for the skins they wore, their own skin was smooth and bare.

The males were larger, more heavily muscled than their females. That did not surprise Oohma. That was true of every pack.

Two of the females held little ones to their breasts with their grimy fingers. Oohma followed the clicks and coos they sang out as their babies sucked them dry.

As he watched, an old one, bent in the legs, with gray on his head, held a shank of bone in his hand and pressed it greedily to his mouth. He turned to the fire's light and Oohma could see that he had just one eye. The other was a thick scar that reached his chin.

Oohma's tongue flicked across his open mouth as the old one put the meaty bone in his, but then Oohma heard the old one howl.

His howls grew louder and louder as he worked on the bone in his mouth. Why would he be howling when he was busy filling his belly with meat? Oohma saw his jaw tighten as he took another savage bite. His ears shot up as a screech shot out of the old one's mouth and pierced the stillness of the night.

The pain drove the old one to his feet and into some sort of wild running and turning that almost put him in the flames. The yelps and screams kept coming but Oohma had stopped watching.

His eyes were on the shank of bone that slipped from the old one's greasy hands and was flying through the night air.

Oohma did not need his eyes to know where it landed. The scent of the charred bone called out to him from the shadows. It was under a thick clump of yellow grasses behind the low-hanging pines.

The old one's good eye swept around in panic as he tore through the brush at the edge of the campsite. He ripped apart the branches. Looked under rocks and kicked at piles of leaves, but Oohma could see that he would never find the bone.

Oohma waited longer than he had to, just to be sure the old one was not moving in the direction of the hidden bone. When he knew it was safe, he jumped to all fours, coiled his powerful legs and sprang forward, taking the bone out of the grass where it landed.

Taking one more look around him, he dropped down and ate it, licking every trace of the juicy bone off his paws and jaw.

Never had meat been so tender. Never had anything been so full of taste, so packed with smell, so full of juice. Every one of Oohma's senses took it in and the ground behind him swirled up into clouds of dust from the sweeping of his tail.

Now he understood why they did it, why moans rolled from their mouths with every chew. Now he knew this would not be the last one. He already wanted more.

CHAPTER 10

After long minutes of crawling and cursing, the old one stood up again, knees bloody and raw. He kicked at the brush, screaming once more before he turned back to the fire, his shoulders slumping.

The others didn't look up or stop their chewing. Loss and hardship were part of their life. All had gone hungry. All had felt pain.

One by one the tribesmen finished feeding and walked off into their shelters to sleep or into the brush to squat. But the one-eyed hunter, even in his pain, had caught a glimpse of red in the night just at the edge of their campsite.

He knew it needed watching and guarding against. Even with his one eye and crooked legs he was still an important hunter, still in touch with his animal spirit. Still in control of his hunter's instincts that had let him reach more than 40 years of life.

A shiver shook the old one's spine as he sat there in the night. He pulled more dried branches from a pile behind him and fed them to the flame. A burst of light leaped up, and the red glow in the underbrush flashed brighter. But this time the hunter saw that it had moved in even closer.

He pushed himself back against the rock wall and drew his knees in tight, his spear next to him. It was going to be a long night with little sleep. But better to keep an eye open than have it closed forever.

Hun, the tribe's leader, still lingered at the fire. He grunted and shrugged his shoulders at Ish, what the one- eyed man was called, and wiped his thick hand across his full belly.

His eyes heavy from the meat and the spiky leaves Lut had given to all, Hun held up the bone and threw it to the old man, then fell into a deep sleep.

Ish didn't hesitate. He grabbed it with hungry hands, put it on the other side of his mouth and tore into it until it was clean. With some meat in his stomach, he sat up straighter and pulled his spear closer to him. Both his brothers had been taken by animals that watched them first, and he was in no hurry to join them.

When morning came and the camp began to stir, Oohma's eyes and ears opened wide to take it all in. He had watched the two-legged ones sleeping on and off through the night. But there was nothing new or strange.

Some he had seen mating off in the shadows, but no different from any he had known. When they moved into the morning sun, their differences came to light.

The fire ate first, before they fed themselves. Once it was alive, the females threw meat on it again. When they had eaten, one of the tribe, the alpha, raised his hand and his voice and clicked something the others seemed to understand. In moments they gathered what they could carry on their backs and in their paws and followed where their leader had pointed.

Following a game trail, they passed under the granite ledge, not even knowing that Oohma was there watching their every move. They couldn't scent what was so close. But Oohma could scent everything even from far away. That made Oohma's tail swish. He was born to stalk and find weaknesses. He'd watch to see if there were more.

CHAPTER 11

They barely moved that day. Three miles, maybe fewer. Oohma's pack could do 30 and more if they had to. There was not an animal in the forest the tribe could outrun or even keep up with or find with their noses.

But as Oohma had observed with growing curiosity, what they could do was more than what they couldn't.

Birds make nests and rabbits dig holes they live inside of. But no other had ever done what Oohma saw these do. Take stones and chip their edges, turning them into sharp blades and axes to take down trees and cover them with thick green branches to sleep inside of. Slash through things with sharp stones. Pull fish from the river using barbed branches. Knock fruit from high trees using tall poles. All these things they did could be done by no other.

As night fell, Oohma edged in even closer. Others of the tribe had seen him and ignored him. But the old one had not. Oohma had seen him look for the flash of his red eyes glowing in the night and the sight of him in the day, off in the distance.

Their eyes had met once quickly. Long enough for something to pass between them. All animals know what they hunt and what hunts them, whether they can live among each other or whether that means death. But the look of the old one and the scents coming off him told Oohma something different. Something he did not yet understand. He sent the pack off to hunt so he could watch and learn.

The tribe had 22, but the only one who mattered to Oohma was the old one. Everywhere he went Oohma tracked him, watching Ish's every move.

He could see that Ish knew how to hunt. But not like the pack. The pack knew where the burrows were. Where their prey hid. How they ran and reacted. Moving together each of them knew their separate role. When to strike and when to circle. When to stay just out of reach and when to move in knowing their target was ready to die.

But Oohma did not see the old hunter join with his pack and circle with them and strike. His old legs would not keep up with the young hunters. So each day Ish struck off on his own, stumbling along, his sharp branch in front of him, hoping his measure of meat would cross his path, close enough to take.

The sun dipped low in the western sky and still the hunter's hands were empty. Oohma could smell the sharp odor of anguish and fear and hunger seeping out of him. The air was heavy with it.

Oohma narrowed his eyes and lifted his nose and the rich scent of game filled it. The old one did not know something good to eat and easy to take was hiding just behind the rocks, just beyond the trees. Oohma knew it without seeing it.

What Oohma didn't know was what the old one would do if he did something to bait him and learn his moves. He knew what the others in the forest did, how they acted, what they ate. Why not this one?

The newborn piglet was close and it was alone. The scent of its mother was farther away, rooting for food on the forest floor.

Oohma moved toward it slowly, careful not to alert the scavenging sow. The piglet didn't look up as Oohma closed in. Its eyes were closed, asleep.

Oohma crouched low and tensed his rear legs. He looked around again, as he always did, to be sure he would not end up on the sow's sharp tusks. In a heartbeat Oohma was in the air.

When he landed the piglet was in his powerful jaws. A quick shake back and forth stopped it from squealing. They would be long gone before the sow got back to her empty nest.

The game trail that the old one followed was easy to find with his sharp nose. He moved down it at half speed, sweeping over the landscape for the scent he knew as an old hunter.

A growing breeze ruffled his fur and the trees around him and Oohma knew right where the old one was. Less than a mile ahead, coming his way.

Oohma tightened his jaws around the piglet and moved farther down the trail, closing in on the one-eyed hunter on high alert for sudden danger.

As he rounded a rock outcropping, Oohma heard the heavy steps of the hunter moving toward him. He stepped out of the shadows and stood, head erect on the trail, as the one- eyed hunter came into view.

The hunter kept coming, but stopped with a start when he saw Oohma standing there. A bolt of fear exploded in his chest. He was heading back empty-handed but the wolf on the trail was not. As all hunters knew, a beast protecting its kill was more dangerous. There was little Ish could do but stand still.

Oohma moved slowly forward, closing the distance between himself and the hunter. The hunter reacted, as Oohma knew he would. He pointed his branch out and pushed his arms out straight.

Step by step, Oohma moved closer, the hair on the scruff of his neck prickling, his ears stiff and erect. Now fewer than 200 steps separated the two of them. Both stopped, watching the other, watching for what the other would do.

Oohma took another few steps and stopped. He opened his jaws and let the piglet fall from his mouth to the trail. Ish's good eye widened. He searched his memory but could remember nothing like it. No animal drops its prey that easily unless it needs its jaws for something else.

Questions flew through him as he stood there trembling. Had he frightened the wolf? Had he startled it, causing it to drop its prey and back away? He needed to be sure his hunger did not steal his caution and cause him to make a move that would turn out to be his last.

Ish swallowed hard and set his feet firmly on the ground, ready to run or fend off the wolf. But the wolf continued backing away. Making no sound. Showing no snarl.

Ish thought for another moment and took another step forward as Oohma watched him and took a step back. Forward and back they went until Ish was closer to the piglet than Oohma was. Keeping his eye on the wolf, Ish carefully lifted the lifeless piglet off the ground.

When the wolf did nothing, Ish turned and ran away as quickly as his old legs would carry him. Looking back over his shoulder more than once, he ran over the hill back to the camp and the safety of the fire.

CHAPTER 12

For days he watched how different they were. In Oohma's pack both males and females joined the hunt. And once pups were weaned they learned quickly and joined in the hunt or at least fended for themselves.

In the tribe the females bore their off-spring and nursed them. Their young could do next to nothing except squeal when they needed to be fed. While at the end of one season, the pack pups were fully grown and self-sufficient, theirs could barely walk and needed to be carried.

Any of his pack could exist alone if they had to, but these needed each other to survive. And the swell in some of their females' bellies showed that the hunters did more than survive. They were growing.

As the sun rose higher above the craggy peaks, Oohma sat up quickly, watching for the one-eyed hunter to come out of his den. Oohma's nose twitched with the first whiffs of smoke from their fires and knew it would not be long.

The scent of the old hunter came to him first. He followed them out of the shadows into the morning light. Oohma could tell them apart now. Each had their own scent, even under the stink they all carried.

He watched the hunters gathered at the fire and listened to them click and nod. His sharp ears were getting used to their sounds. When they stood up and reached for their pointed branches all but Ish moved in a pack. He went off in his own direction and let the others go in theirs.

Oohma did not follow any of the others, even with a look. When the one-eyed hunter disappeared, limping over the rim of a hill, Oohma trailed after him. Far enough back so he would not be seen but close enough to see all that the old one would do.

Oohma watched his gait, heard his outbursts of pain and smelled the struggles of his body climbing among the rocks. Hunger had sent him out to find a nest filled with eggs low enough to reach. The piglet was long gone and the old hunter's belly was growling.

The crackle of dried leaves snapped Oohma's head back as a fat rabbit moved across it. What would the old one do? What more would Oohma learn about him if he dropped the rabbit in his path?

Staying low, staying quiet, he dropped on all fours letting the rabbit be led by its hunger not its ears. When it was close enough to take, Oohma took it in one leap.

The rabbit didn't know it was happening until it already had. It froze in a desperate attempt to blend into the background but it was too late. One second later, the rabbit was up in the air, its warm blood trickling down from Oohma's mouth.

CHAPTER 13

Ish stumbled along the trail cursing his empty hand. The meaty bone given by Hun and the fat, young piglet dropped by the wolf had been gifts of the gods or fate. But luck did not show its face often. Why would it come again?

A rustle behind him made the old hunter's heart jump and spun him around. He squinted, covering his one good eye from the sun. And then he saw it. Something was moving at him, but what it was he could not yet tell.

Oohma knew that the old hunter had seen him. Still he kept on coming, head down, tail tucked, ears tight against his body. A signal of submissiveness not aggression, he hoped the old one would know.

When Ish saw it was Oohma, the wolf he had encountered before, he backed up a bit, as curious as he was frightened. But this time he did not raise his pointed branch.

Oohma came steadily closer and the old hunter could not believe his eye. Prey was in his reach again. All he had to do was take the rabbit from the wolf's mouth.

The two of them stood there locked in each other's eyes, looking across a divide that had been since the beginning of time. Each species living in its own ways, among its own kind, coming together when they were either the hunter or the hunted.

Ish stepped back, careful to keep some space between them and gazed with bewilderment into Oohma's golden eyes. At any other time, in any other place, the locking of eyes was a challenge meant to be answered with conflict and blood. But all they did was look.

With a flick of his head Oohma dropped the rabbit. Instead of racing away he backed up, opening a small space between them. A strange look crossed Ish's face. What was he seeing? Was the wolf the spider and he the fly? Had a trap been baited for him to fall into?

Oohma could scent the thoughts whirling around him. He could see them twist his face and wrinkle his brow. He could hear his labored breath. But then Oohma heard his breathing slow and the lines on his face go softer as a simple thing came to the old hunter. If the wolf had wanted to take him, wouldn't he already be dead?

The hunter gathered his courage and put his hand on the slender stone knife. With his eye riveted on Oohma, he drew it out. The shine of its black obsidian blade glinted in the sun as he held it up, just in case.

Oohma's eyes never left the old hunter. He kept his distance, still not sure of what the old one and his pointed stones might do. But his were not the only eyes that were watching. The forest crawled with predators, their powerful senses always searching for an easy bite.

Ish moved for the rabbit before the wolf changed its mind, but something moved even faster. Hungry and angry, it woke to fresh scents on the trail. An old man and a dead rabbit, both easy targets, and a wolf nowhere near its thousand pounds of strength and fury.

Time froze as the three of them, Oohma, the hunter and the bear took each other in, measuring the threat before them. Nothing moved until the bear did. Three long lunges put it on the old man's back, driving him brutally to the ground, shrieking in pain and fear. Ish punched wildly and kicked at the bear as hard as he could, desperate to shield his vulnerable body from its gruesome claws.

Neither Ish nor the bear heard Oohma's paws pounding as he ran. Neither saw his powerful jaws open, baring his snarling teeth. Neither saw him spring into the air.

The pain jolted the bear like a bolt of lightning, making it leap off the old one's back as Oohma's razor-sharp fangs found the bones of its claw.

The bear shot straight up as Oohma bit down harder. Its bellows drowned out Ish's shrieks as it tried to shake Oohma off. But Oohma would not let go no matter how many times the bear slammed his body into the ground.

The bear spun wildly, crashing into the huge stones around it, but it did no good. Oohma didn't stop biting until the bear backed off and limped off howling down the trail, its severed paw left behind in Oohma's mouth.

Oohma dropped the paw and leaped for the old man, pulling him to an open place where he could sense if he had gotten to him in time.

Oohma's hot breath on Ish's bloody face made the old man groan and slowly open his eye, certain he had died. When it focused enough for him to see he was not in the clouds but on the ground, he saw Oohma standing over him, deep gashes and bloody clumps dripping from his furry coat.

And he saw something far beyond it. The pig and the rabbit weren't the only gifts the wolf had given him. This time it had been his life.

Before he could stop himself or think it through, he reached out for Oohma and gently stroked his deep wounds. Oohma let him even though the pain ripped through him with every touch.

The rabbit was still where Oohma had dropped it. Oohma pushed at it with his nose until it was next to Ish's feet. Ish picked it up and made his way toward the flat stone behind him, wincing with each step.

Throwing the rabbit down, Ish pulled out his knife and sliced the rabbit in two. He put one piece in his sack, then threw the other to Oohma.

It landed with a thud a few inches from Oohma's face. The old one pointed his shaggy chin at it, signaling for Oohma to take his share. Tail tucked between his legs, body slumped, Oohma let him know he would.

CHAPTER 14

Ish returned to the campsite racked with pain, but with a newfound energy and fresh meat in his sack once more. He looked around. Hun and the other hunters were nowhere to be seen.

The women of the tribe, busy at their tasks, barely looked up when he passed them. More intent on the baskets of rough fronds they were weaving, they stopped only to throw the palm scraps on the still smoldering ashes of the fire.

He clicked at one of them, a female of 19 but already showing the ravages of time. She sat off in a shady corner, a child at her breast, a basket in her lap. Her eyes found his and she tilted her chin in the direction of the valley below. Ish understood her meaning. Hun and the tribesman were down there, still on the hunt.

Spent, Ish let his head fall back against the rough stone, a strange look on his face and a strange thought in his head. The survival of the tribe had always been shared by all. As was the hunt, as was the meat, with no thought to who took it. It was enough that it was taken and could be eaten.

Still, if the hunters came home empty-handed again, he had not. And that would make what he had in his sack even more valuable, giving him what he valued most. The place of honor at the fire he had lost with his eye.

He sat stone-faced as he came to a decision. He would share the rabbit as he did the piglet, but not how he got it. Not until he understood what had happened between him and the wolf.

When the sun began to sink into the western sky, Ish took up a post at the head of the trail. His head was pounding along with his heart. Something of great power and mystery had dropped in his lap and it was far greater than the rabbit. No beast had ever reached out to him and saved his life. No powerful forest predator had ever shared its meat or let him get close enough to touch it.

Night arrived by the time the hunters did, but even in the dim light the sag of their shoulders told the story. They returned with nothing once again.

Ish waited until the hunters sat huddled around the fire, chewing on nuts and berries, before he went to retrieve his sack.

No one looked when he did, but when he returned, their eyes popped wide open. The old one carried the meat of rabbit. A ravenous look crossed their faces as they watched Ish limp up to Hun and drop it in his lap.

Hun did nothing for a moment but look up at Ish, one hand on the rabbit and one hand on his chin. No one moved or made a sound. Only the crackle of the fire, the rush of the river and the chirping of the crickets kept on.

After a breathless moment, Hun lifted his thick body and shifted himself to the left, leaving an open place at the fire.

Ish didn't move right away. He just stood there rocking back and forth, looking down at the tribe leader. Hun clicked and gestured again, patting the empty spot on the hard dirt beside him. Ish waited, savoring the moment as he would the rabbit, before he nodded his shaggy head and sat down.

Hours before, the females led by Lut had foraged out far and wide, returning with nuts and seeds and grains, wild carrots and tubers and cattails that grew in a bog. Even without meat the tribe would survive. But it was the densely packed proteins of meat that allowed them to thrive and the sight of it made their mouths go wet.

Ish took the rabbit back and handed it to one of the women of the tribe making sure all were watching. With flying fingers she stripped its pelt and dropped the bloody meat into the hollow of a round stone the toolmaker had turned into a deep bowl.

A measure of water from a gourd and handfuls of leafy greens Lut had slashed from the earth were added to the hollow. Next came purple carrots and fragrant white bulbs. A handful of grain followed.

Once the cooking bowl was filled almost to the top, Lut carried it to the flame. Another of the females moved to help her position it over the embers.

All had their jobs. Some stepped out for wood, some stood still and stirred as the stew began to boil and the air filled with its smell.

When it smelled the way Lut wanted, she nodded and the women scooped out measures of the rich stew onto wide green leaves. Hun snatched his greedily but stopped before he began to eat, handing it to Ish instead.

The tradition of the tribe existed before any of them did and it had to be honored. The one who fed them ate first.

CHAPTER 15

Ish set out early before any of the other males had woken from their sleep. He picked his way carefully past the snoring bodies, his hand pressed against the walls of the rock outcropping for support. Glancing over his shoulder, he quietly left the camp, a sense of anticipation tingling through his body.

The last days had been filled with wonders and he wondered what might be coming next. Everything was happening so quickly he could not guess. Better, he knew, to keep his eye and his mind open. He had been gifted with fresh meat twice before by a beast that should have killed him. That was enough to think about.

Oohma jumped up and disappeared into the forest. He trailed carefully behind the old hunter, staying far enough away so that he would not be seen. The forest was thick with trees and brush and alive with the early morning calls of insects chewing on the tender leaves of trees.

Beech, oak, firs, pines, junipers crowded in on each other, reaching up for the sunlight of the warming sky.

Closer to the earth, shorter, squatter trees held olives and plums, apples and pears on their slender branches.

Birds picked at them as the fruits ripened and the buzz of bees could be heard sipping at their blossoms. Many of them Ish did not know, had never seen or tasted before and was not sure if they brought pleasure or pain and death.

The tribe had always followed prey and the rush of rivers with no planned route in mind. This place they had stumbled upon was not yet fully known. Even their hunting parties had only ventured out a few miles from their camp. Not wanting to be trapped in the dark in a forest full of death.

Oohma and his pack had explored the landscape for miles around, as they did with every place they stopped. What their eyes could not see their noses could find. Even those faraway vines hanging high in the canopy, heavy with grapes. And even the papery hives buzzing with stinging bees that hung down a little lower.

Oohma's nose knew how good their taste would be the first time their sweet scent found him. But the hives had always been too high to get to. And if a hive was on the ground, having fallen, the angry warnings of bees kept them from getting close enough to take it.

The old hunter had some tricks he could do with his two front paws, if Oohma could get him to use them to swipe at one. Oohma's gift had been shared before. Why would it not be shared again?

The old hunter sensed something around him and drew in a sharp breath as he turned his head. It caught in his throat as he saw the wolf again, just a hundred or so feet away.

Ish moved back a few steps when he saw the wolf coming, not sure of what might happen. He gripped his stone point tightly in his hand, ready if he had to. Trust was not given easily, for good reason.

Oohma could sense the old man's feelings. Fear has a scent he knew well. But so does curiosity and the old man had both. Oohma kept his pace steady and came in even closer, closing the gap even tighter between animal and man.

Oohma took the last few feet in one graceful leap. Ish felt his heart leap as Oohma closed his jaw on his wrist. The blood drained from his face, but Oohma just held him, no pressure, no pain. Two heartbeats and he gave Ish a tug, pulling him toward the trail behind them. All throughout, Oohma's ears stayed smoothed down against his lowered head, yielding.

When he was sure Ish understood what he wanted him to do, he dropped his arm and walked slowly enough for Ish to follow. A stand of pines stretched out to the left of them.

A tall dead one was alive with a high-pitched buzzing sound. The end of a drooping branch held a beehive low enough for Ish to get to with a pole.

At the bottom of a short hill, just a few feet down, a small stream washed by. The mossy rocks along its sides held pools of deeper water. Oohma knew exactly what to do when he saw them, but he was not sure Ish did.

Three times he raced from the hive to the stream and back, splashing his paws in the deeper pools, then running back to Ish to look into his eyes. He saw from the way Ish moved and the clicking sound he had gotten used to hearing that Ish finally understood.

Picking up a long branch, Ish walked up to the tree while Oohma took a few steps back. Ish took a steadying breath and then a hard swing with the branch. Silence. An angry buzzing exploded as it hit the ground and rolled.

Ish moved quickly, jamming at the nest until it began to roll down the hill. He dunked it into a deep pool and kept it there until the bees in the sky scattered and the ones in the hive floated up to the water's surface. Ish speared it out.

Shock and joy flashed across his face as he held the dripping nest on a pole. Like the piglet and the rabbit, this could not have happened without the wolf.

His head was spinning as he stabbed his finger into the nest and drew out a comb dripping with honey. He put some in his mouth and held out a fingerful. Oohma came forward and licked his hand. Then when Ish bent down he licked his face. The old man pulled back when he felt Oohma's warm tongue on his gruff face. But then Oohma did it again and a wave of warmth filled the old man's body. Moments passed as they stood there locked in each other's eyes speaking things that needed no words.

Ish put the hive on the end of the branch and a hand on Oohma's head. He could feel the warmth of his coat and the strength of his body. He liked how it felt to feel Oohma press against him when he walked with him.

Together they walked back down the trail, side by side for the first time, and Ish felt a strange tingle. His hand on Oohma's head did not feel strange at all. It felt like it had always been there and Oohma had always been there right at his side.

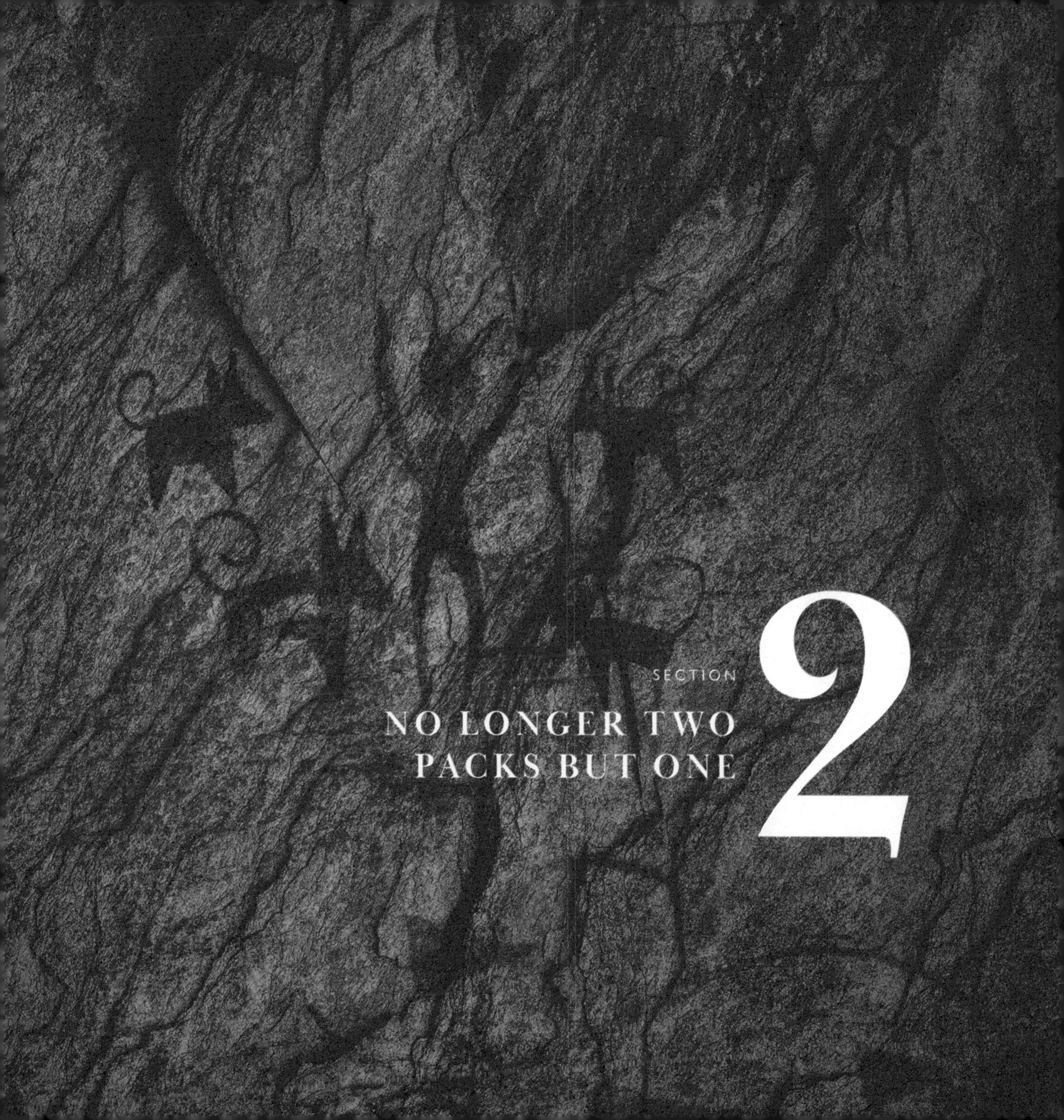

SECTION 2

NO LONGER TWO PACKS BUT ONE

CHAPTER 16

Oohma left the old hunter when the scent of the tribe reached him on the wind. He climbed back to his perch in the high rocks and hid under the brush.

His pack went wild when one of them brought down game.

Would the old one's pack do the same with the honey inside the hive? Oohma lay down to watch.

Ish took his time coming up to the fire, waiting until every eye was on him. He reached into his sack and pulled out a dripping honeycomb. Their jaws fell open at the sight.

Ish broke off a hunk and handed it to Hun. Hun's instincts overtook his pride and he grabbed at it with a nod.

Ish walked around breaking off pieces and giving one to every one of the tribe. The only sounds that could be heard were moans of joy. Hun finished his in seconds and licked his hands and lips until nothing was left of the honey but the memory of its taste.

Ish stood over him letting it be understood by all as the mighty Hun sat at his feet. The moment was sweet and Ish looked hard at each of them until each looked away. Then he dangled another chunk of honeycomb just inches beyond Hun's reach.

Hun reached out to grab it but he lost his balance and pitched forward on his knees instead. Ish waited another beat, staring down as Hun crawled towards him, grabbing for his arm. But Ish stayed just far enough away.

Finally, when he knew that all the tribe had seen Hun grovel at his feet, he let Hun get close enough to take the comb from his hands.

The next morning before the sun rose, Oohma watched Ish come out of his den and walk to the fire. His ears dropped when he heard the old man moan in pain as he struggled to straighten his back. Oohma could tell that the pain grew worse each time the old one headed out.

When he straightened up with a final grunt, Ish shook his head to drive out the strange images that had swirled through him and kept him from sleep all night.

In them he was young again, racing with the wind, but he was not alone. A sleek gray wolf paced him at his side. It hunted with him, racing down prey, driving it back at Ish so he could get close enough with his spear to take it down.

Oohma had done more than come out of the forest. He had crawled inside of Ish, even into his dreams.

More than once Ish's dreams had talked. And more than once they had told him things worth knowing. But this thing that had come to him had never been worth even thinking. This was not hunting an animal as he had always done. This was hunting with an animal. And that had never been done.

Lut heard Ish pacing and muttering and came outside. She waited a moment, then came up and stood in front of him.

Their language was crude and in need of new words to communicate all that they had seen and encountered. Still Ish could see the questions on Lut's face.

He had known since it happened that soon the questions would be asked. How had he, an old hunter with one good eye and two bad legs, become the great one again, returning over and over with game and treasure when the other hunters, younger, stronger, faster, could not?

When it grew light enough to move into the forest, Ish motioned for Lut to follow. Too many things were happening to keep it to himself anymore. And Lut with her powers and skills was the only one who could understand and be trusted.

Lut knew it was something important and followed him quietly down the trail to the place Ish and Oohma usually found each other.

The moment they stopped, a loud noise burst from behind and Oohma leaped out onto the trail. His golden eyes swept over Lut and he pulled in streams of air before he came any closer. He knew Lut from her scent but only from afar.

Lut jumped back in terror, pressing herself hard into a tree and covering her face, waiting to die. She waited another moment and then another, but still she was alive.

Ish put his hands on her shoulders and she slowly opened her eyes. He tapped on her and made a gesture that said, *Do not worry, everything is alright.*

Still Ish had to pull her forward with all of his strength, and while he did he reached out and put his other hand on Oohma's head.

Lut looked hard at Ish snapping her head back in disbelief. Finally she relented and let Ish bring her to Oohma.

Lut gazed deeply into Oohma's golden eyes opening herself to whatever the fates would bring. Only inches between them and thousands of years of instinct telling her to run.

Fear was not an enemy but a friend. It was why Lut still walked the earth, why she still breathed. So it took all her courage to put it aside and put herself in Ish's hands.

She had never been this close to a predator before unless it was chasing her. Or it was hunted and being dragged to the flames. She heard her grandmother's voice whisper as she often did, even from the clouds.

"Only new things can teach you. What you know has already been told."

Lut knew Nuun's words could be trusted. The moment was proof of that. She was standing close enough to a killer to feel its breath on her neck and she was still standing.

Oohma put his face near hers. She could feel his energy surround her as she let him. She steadied herself and reached out her trembling hand.

FIRST DOG ON EARTH

Oohma's coat was soft to her touch. Her panic melted away when he leaned against her letting her feel his warmth. She stroked him softly up and down setting his tail free. When she saw it she chirped a happy sound.

Oohma circled them twice. He knew it was time and moved down the trail. Just as Ish had kept the wolf a secret from his pack, so had Oohma from his. But the time had come to change that. His pack stayed at the den without straying, waiting for Oohma's return. They were on their paws when the scent of Oohma and the two that were with him arrived.

Oohma looked back at Ish and froze. Ish understood Oohma's meaning and reached for Lut's arm, pulling her back toward him while Oohma raced ahead to his pack.

They stood perfectly still, their ears erect, waiting for what Oohma wanted of them. Oohma circled them once, pressing them into a tight pack. One by one, he rubbed his body against them. Pressing the smell of Ish and Lut into their coats and making it part of them.

Each of the pack sniffed at themselves and then each other, taking in the new scents up close. Oohma circled the pack. A hard stare told them what they were to do.

Their nostrils flared and the hair on the scruff of their necks stood up as they rounded the hill and Ish and Lut came into view.

Their hearts were pumping fast, pushing them into attack mode, but Oohma's fierce look restrained them.

He led the pack forward. Ish who had grown confident around Oohma fell back in terror as all six of the wolves stood just a pounce away.

Knowing how closely the pack was watching, Oohma walked calmly up to the old male first and then to the female and rubbed against them.

The pack watched with shock, fear and excitement, but Oohma was their leader and they stood still. Still they could not keep themselves quiet. Some growled, some snarled, some let out low barks.

One by one, Oohma calmed them and led each up to the old man and then to the young girl, letting them encounter each other for the first time.

The pack was anxious, sniffing hard at the old man and the girl. But after some moments passed they smelled no anger and followed Oohma's lead and settled down, just circling the two of them again and again.

After Lut's heart stilled she found her courage and reached out and stroked each one of them with a gentle hand and cooing sounds as she had done to Oohma.

Ish followed and in that moment all eight, the six wolves and the two humans, were no longer two packs but one.

CHAPTER 17

CHAPTER 18

Ish and Lut rounded the low hill and picked their way down the rocky incline as they did every day. But this day was different. Different from any that had ever been. Lut and Ish were walking toward them but they were not alone.

Six wolves were calmly padding with them, pressed tightly together as a pack. Not attacking them. Not stalking them. But walking calmly at their side, with Lut and Ish stroking them as they did.

Every sound, every breath at the campsite stopped. Whatever was in their hands or arms came crashing to the ground. It was as if time itself had stopped. The tribesmen looked around quickly, not knowing what to do, waiting for Ish or Lut or Hun to tell them.

A moment passed, maybe two, before the tribe gathered their wits and reached for their weapons. Their eyes darted back and forth between Lut and Ish, then back to Hun again, waiting for an order. Hun moved first. If the old man wouldn't, he would.

Positioning his spear he waited for what was to come. His mind raced along with his pulse. The medicine woman could not be lost or they would be, and the old man had become a meat source again and that could not be squandered. Hun pressed the shaft of his spear tightly against his body and led the tribe carefully forward.

Ish and Lut leaped out in front of them shrieking and waving their arms. But the tribe did not stop, with Hun urging them on.

Lut didn't wait. She raced at Hun slamming her arms into his chest. It took all her strength but finally she pushed him back.

Hun's eyes were wild with confusion. What to think, what to do? He could not understand what Ish and Lut were saying. There was a pack of killer wolves at their backs. What else could be done but attack or run?

Lut's head slashed back and forth and she let out a piercing sound, harsh and abrupt. Hun knew what that meant. *Stop. Wait. Listen.* And Lut had never been wrong. But still there had never been a moment like it. Their medicine woman was protecting a pack of predators from her own.

Attack was surging through Hun's veins. His legs were coiled and his fists were tightened into stones, almost beyond his control. But finally he let Lut lower his arm along with his spear.

Had any of the tribe done that, no less a female, he would have flattened them with the back of his hand. But Hun knew he could not. Lut's powers had become too great. And Hun knew deep in his soul that if it came down to a choice between him and her, the tribe would choose the medicine girl.

Lut breathed in deeply and closed her eyes, waiting to feel the power flow through her. When she felt it and felt in control of the moment again she reached out gently and put her hand on Hun's shoulder.

Her eyes drilled into him and her face softened as she pulled him into the center of the pack. Ish stood back and watched the world change around him.

Hun swallowed hard. Drawing a whistling breath he let Lut put his shaking hand on Oohma's soft head. Oohma looked up, closed his mouth and let him. But then he shook Hun's hand off his head and stepped back, letting the rest of the tribe come pet him instead.

Walking slowly, at a comfortable pace, Lut and Ish led the pack and tribe back to the campsite. The sky was darkening as they reached it.

As the women stoked the fires, Ish stroked each of the pack as he walked among them. Hun went to the spot he slept in and crawled inside. When he came out he held a soft skin in his hand. Inside it was a special blade, shaped by an elder in the years before they lived, the symbol of power and position.

Hun walked up to Ish, head lowered, shoulders sagging. With a swift move he pulled the blade out of the skin and handed it to Ish. What once he had lost Ish now took back. He took it with a nod and tied the sheaf to his waist. Then he sat down at the head of the fire, the leader's place once again.

The pack stood a distance off but the hunks of meat Ish handed to Oohma brought them in close. Soon the pack joined in and both fed together as though they always had. They settled down to sleep for the night and be ready to hunt in the morning.

CHAPTER 19

Oohma kept the pack close to the tribe now. Following his lead they dug dens out of the dirt face of the hill, above the campsite, and made it their home and their territory. They began sharing the meat from their hunts with the ones they had taken into their pack.

It had taken a while for the tribe, other than Ish and Lut, to accept the wolves among them. Their primal fears lived too deep inside, as they did with many of the pack. Both were ready to bolt in a second, especially when the fire was roaring and near.

Oohma was different. His fear of the flames lessened each night as his trust in Lut and Ish grew. Fire was part of the tribe and he and the pack were now part of the tribe, so Oohma accepted it along with its warmth and his meat.

The meat they shared filled Oohma's stomach. But it was something else that filled him, something that was warm and soothing like the sunshine on his coat or the fire's glow. It was inside him and he felt it run through him when Ish and Lut were near him. When their hands were on him, rubbing him and ruffling his fur. When their eyes met and softened and they pressed against each other. Oohma could get his own meat, but that feeling? There was only one way to get that. Ish or Lut.

On mornings when Ish did not emerge from his hut, his strength and energy too low to hunt, Oohma would head out with Lut and lead her to places she had never known or explored before. And each time Lut followed Oohma she would return with strange new treasures to enrich the tribe's health and enrich her status even more.

Oohma kept his head close to Lut as they moved along the trail. There was something special about her now. Oohma could sense a subtle shift in the scent he had come to know.

She, like the females of his pack, was coming into her time, though it did not yet show. Was Ish aware of that? Was Lut his mate? Oohma would watch them closely and sniff around them and then he would know.

Most nights he sat between Lut and Ish moving his head from one to the other and nuzzling his long nose into their necks. Never before had the neck of a human in the jaws of a wolf brought such feelings of pleasure for both.

Each time Oohma snuggled in close, licking the sweat on Ish's salty neck, a strange sound burst from the old one's mouth. An outburst of air that sounded like "ha" repeated over and over again. And each time it did Ish rubbed Oohma's back even harder, ruffling his fur and patting his head until Oohma's tail swept the dirt clean behind him.

When it did, all the tribesmen banged their spears on the hard earth and their females let out whoops and spun in circles at the wonder of it all. At the wolf pack that now lived among them and brought them meat every night. But one did not.

Hun sat off in a shadowy corner, his anger sharper than the points he made for his spear. He turned away as the tribesmen banged their spears and their females whooped and spun themselves into dizziness near the fire.

Let them bang their spears, he cursed to himself as chips of flint flew from his hands. *Let them just make their own.*

A band of dark clouds clustered in the eastern sky and opened with fury above the campsite, driving the tribe and the pack under a rock shelf. Claps of thunder crashed above them and streaks of lightening crossed the sky as Ish dropped to one knee, calling them in close.

This thing that he thought had been with him for years as they roamed the earth, always moving to stay alive, it could never have been till now. A place the tribe could stay and not move from, that could feed them well because of how well the pack could hunt.

Oohma watched the tribesmen's faces as the old one bent and scratched a circle in the dirt. Their looks and the scent of them told Oohma they were confused.

They all had wandered since the day of their births. There was no home, just places they stopped at hoping to find game. There was no other way to live but to follow the food. Oohma and the pack changed that.

Inside the wide circle Ish scratched out a tight cluster of huts that could be made easily from the thin trunks of young trees, tied at their tops with strips of hide and covered all over with skins. Not the branch-covered huts the wind howled through and the rain leaked into.

A silence swept over them as Ish's vision sunk in. They were to stay where they were? No more endlessly walking until weariness knocked them down? No more having to seek new shelters or fight predators for caves each night?

One by one the silence was broken as a grunting began to fill the air. To have a space of their own to return to each day and sleep in each night, warm and dry. What else could that be but good?

When morning came, driving the rain away with a warming sun, Oohma sat up and watched the tribesman go into the forest and attack the trees with the sharpened stones they swung with their front paws.

It took strike after strike and scream after scream, sometimes blood from their paws, but the trees soon fell at their feet. Once they had taken enough, they stripped them of leaves and branches and stood them up again, gathered and tied them at the top with narrow strips of vine.

When the males were finished, the females stepped in, dragging softened animal hides behind them along with sharpened bones and lengths of twine made from twisted grasses.

The bones of the tents soon took on skins as the females wrapped and sewed them tight, leaving just a slit at the front to let them go in and out.

One after another the huts went up, the first for Ish. But Ish shook his head and held his hands out in front of him. No, his head said and he stepped aside, giving it to Lut. Taking the second for himself and all took its meaning. Lut was revered above all others, even the leader of the tribe.

The pack had always lived differently. They roamed. They hunted. They ate and slept. Made nothing but the softened spot they slept in. No plans. No things. No tomorrow. Just the day they woke up to.

The tribe needed shelters if they wanted to survive, and the leathery hides they took along with the meat would make that happen. Oohma sat off in the shade watching. When the skins were tight around Lut and Ish's tents, a young male Ish called Baba, with a thin, delicate body and a pleasant, easy face, walked up to Ish's hut with a stick in his hand. The stick bled red from its end, but it made no sound of pain.

From the time Baba was old enough to walk, the tribe could see what he could do with his hands. But they could also see that he saw what others of the tribe didn't. That his look went beyond what he was looking at, letting him look into them and draw out the essence of what lived inside them along with their shapes.

When other little ones took sticks and stones and dragged them across the ground leaving behind crude lines and circles, Baba scratched trees and flowers and birds flapping away in the sky.

On the day Baba scratched down a face with tussled hair and a thin grim mouth that looked so much like Hun, all knew in a second who it was. All knew what the others were thinking.

Baba didn't need to hunt. They would feed him and he would draw more and draw in more of the animals in his own special way, with the gift the gods had given him.

For long minutes Oohma cocked his head back and forth as Baba waved his hand in front of the skin. He looked like he was trying to draw something out of it, something he knew was hiding inside.

Oohma's jaw opened wide. A menacing growl shot out as Baba dragged the stick over the skin and a bison, its head and horns raised up high, jumped out of Baba's hand and stampeded across the stretched skin of the tent. What magic was this? Who could make a bison come alive out of blood and piss and berries?

Oohma's snout wrinkled in terror as he sniffed at the air, but the scent of bison was nowhere. Just the familiar scent of Baba, the red juice of berries and blood and the bleeding red end of a stick.

Each stroke of red brought others to life. Lions, horses, bears and gazelles, their legs in flight as they galloped across the tent, making no noise, raising no dust, causing no stink.

Could he trust his eyes no more? Why could his nose not find anywhere what his eyes could plainly see right in front of him on the skins of the tent?

CHAPTER 20

It had rained steadily through the night, soaking the skins above her. The dampness she felt on her night tunic didn't catch her attention until she saw its color. A spot of dark crimson on her light tan hide.

She clenched her teeth but still she cried out in joy. It was the sign she and the tribe had been watching for. The medicine girl was now the medicine woman.

With the moment came the expectations. Every female of the tribe was expected to bear fruit, especially a medicine woman whose offspring would be instructed in the healing ways. No tribe could exist without children. They were as vital as food itself. But the children of a medicine woman? They would be born full of magic.

Since the days before they could remember, the leader of the tribe was first to plant his seed. But the leader was now a grizzled, one-eyed ancient, not a young strong man like Hun. Each of the tribe felt what Lut was feeling. Even with no words it was painted all over their faces.

As night fell and the fire burned low, the tribe began to drift. Only Ish and Lut stayed behind. Lut watched Ish intensely, but each time their eyes met Ish looked away. What he would have relished as a younger man hung like a weight around his neck. But he could wait no longer.

Ish stood up and reached down for Lut, taking her hand. She could read his thoughts and shared his sadness as they walked toward Ish's tent. Her first night as a woman should have been a celebration. Instead it filled her with anguish and dread.

Inside Ish's tent a small flame gave enough light for both of them to see. Ish took Lut and gently sat her down on a mat of straw. He dropped his head with a sigh, loosened the leather strap around his waist and let his loincloth fall.

A sad and sour look etched his face. His spirit was willing but his body was not. A shiver of sadness shook him as he looked at Lut. There was nothing to be said.

Lut said nothing, but neither did she look away. She waited a few moments, then put her finger across her lips. "Shhhh," she hissed as she bent down to pull his loincloth up. When he was dressed again she touched his face, stepped around him and walked to the opening of the tent.

Lut waited a long moment. Then she opened the tent flap just a sliver and let out a piercing scream followed by a series of cries, sharp and short. The tribesmen who passed Ish's tent nodded as they heard them.

Ish and Lut were obeying the first rule of the tribe, helping it to grow. In the morning she would find an answer and Ish would not have lost his pride.

Sleep did not find her as it had found Ish. Somewhere just beyond her reach something was gnawing at her, keeping her awake. She calmed her breathing and clamped her eyelids shut. Whispers were reaching out for her.

Waves of color flowed out of the darkness and swirled around her, bursts of purple and explosions of white. When they cleared, a herd of wild goats chewing on grasses came into her vision. Some, the larger males in the herd, drifted off to the sides.

They stopped at a cluster of tall purple flowers growing at the edge of the meadow and began to chew them to the ground. Once they did, their bodies spiked with energy, making them streak across the field. The females looked up from the grass they were feeding on and prepared to withstand the males that were coming to mount their backs.

Lut heard the flowers whisper to her, "Watch the goats."

CHAPTER **21**

It was not yet dawn and the camp was silent, just the wind in the trees and Lut stirring inside Ish's tent. Oohma was up on all fours the moment he heard her and padded down to meet her at the tent. She reached down to scratch his head and when he came up to her he raised his nose, poking it between her thighs. He cocked his head to one side as he backed away a few feet and held Lut in his eyes.

Lut had been with Ish throughout the night, yet Ish's scent was not on her. She was in flower but her petals were still intact. Something a female in his pack would never be. Not when the season was upon them and the scent was making the males pounce on the females' backs.

Oohma circled Lut a few times and started off down the trail. It was a signal that had grown between them that Lut knew well. It meant, Follow.

Below the camp a rushing stream cut through a mossy landscape. Lut followed Oohma along its bank, careful not to slide down one of the slippery rocks that bordered the small ribbon of water. A broken leg or a fracture, even for a medicine woman, could be life's end.

Oohma crossed the stream and waited for Lut. She grabbed a fallen branch and used it to help her cross. On the flat of land above the stream the trees thickened, blocking out the sky and turning the day a shade of night.

Oohma moved through them toward a block of light at the end of the tree line, looking back often to be sure Lut was not in danger.

The break in the trees widened to reveal a meadow below. Wild goats fed on its lush grasses while the larger males grazed on the bright purple flowers growing in profusion along its edge.

Lut shook her head and made an ummmmm sound that brought a haha out of her. She'd seen it all before in her visions and somehow Oohma knew it. But Oohma knew what animals do, even when Lut did not.

Once the larger males had eaten their fill of the flowers and went to drink from a shallow pond, they reared up and bucked on their rear legs. Kicking and snorting filled the air.

Hearing Lut and Oohma coming toward them, the goats scattered, clumps of torn flowers still in their mouths.

Lut had her bag open before they reached the purple flowers. Once there she tore at them, gathering up armfuls of the plants, flowers, roots and stems. She stuffed them in her bag.

She knew what she would do with them when they returned to camp. Boil the stems and roots in water to make a tea for Ish to drink and give him the petals to chew on.

While Lut gathered the flowers, Oohma sniffed them and chewed on a stem, then sniffed at them again and again. Was there anything else with a scent like that near by?

Oohma pulled in the air and scurried up a hill, his nose running along the ground as though he were tracking a mole. He stopped when he came to a low green plant with a red flower above it and started to dig.

Lut heard dirt flying and hurried up the hill. Oohma had led her to treasures before and she did not hesitate now. By the time she reached him, Oohma stood on a pile of loose dirt, his nose covered with it, and his mouth held a pale yellow root that looked like a two-legged carrot, about eight inches long.

Lut took the root from him and turned it in her hand, brushing aside the clumps of dirt stuck to it. The plant was unknown. She made her haha sound as she got to know it.

It was like a little male, with two legs, and where the legs came together, a little stem stuck out. Lut looked at Oohma and patted his head, then dug for more.

When she had as many as she could carry, she put them in her bag. There were other small green growths that came out with the yellow root, some still attached to the seeds they grew out of. The thought of what she was seeing blew her eyes wide open as she held one up in the sun.

Claps of thunder don't always happen in the sky.

CHAPTER **22**

Lut hoisted the heavy sack onto her back and followed Oohma back to the campsite. As she and Oohma rounded the hill, the other females rushed out to meet her, but Lut pushed them away. What she had found was not for them, not yet. Not until she knew more, not until the time was right.

Lut often held things back that she was unsure of, but this time it was more than the welfare of the tribe. This was much more personal.

Her hopes ran as high as her intuition. Still, a shudder of fear. Everyone had seen the lust and anger in Hun's eyes and the disappointment he could not hide when she entered the hut with Ish. All knew to steer wide and clear of Hun. Even a look his way could unleash his wrath.

Medicine woman or not, the tribe's survival depended on new blood, new beings, new lives to replace the old. If Ish could not fill Lut with child, someone else would have to and she knew who that would be.

Once she was inside the hut, Lut pulled the skin across the opening and tied it shut. In the dim light she emptied the sack. She carefully separated the flowers, the stems and the roots. But the strange green shoots sticking out of the hard black seeds, those she carefully put aside.

The sharp stone knife and her skillful hands split the root in half with one stroke. Flat side down, she picked up a long smooth stone made to fit her hand and crushed the fibrous root into a paste. She dipped her finger into it.

The taste of the ginseng root was full of earth and spice. It made her tongue tingle but not go numb. Lut set a hollowed stone near the glowing fire. She watched and waited until a plume of steam rose up from the water. When it did, she stirred in a handful of crushed root and let it sit until the water turned a cloudy yellow.

Lut poured the hot water through a reed basket and let the liquid fill the hollow of another gourd. When she was satisfied enough time had passed, she took the softened pulp and squeezed out every drop she could, then placed it on a wide green leaf to cool.

She'd feed Ish the pulp with a generous portion of meat to make him strong. Then she'd give him the brew to swallow, along with the petals of the purple flowers and their stems.

Three times each day she gave Ish her cure. She kept him on his fur mat making him rest all day. Ish did what Lut told him to and ate and drank what she brought him.

For three nights there was nothing. But on the fourth night she felt him stir and his energy spike as he turned to her. Finally his old body had come back to life.

Once they had obeyed the traditions of the tribe and become mates, Ish's eye shut again and his breathing deepened as sleep returned to him. But Lut's did not. Still she stayed quiet and drew in life's energy, willing her body to accept Ish's gift.

As she lay there, she whispered to the spirits and reached out for her grandmother Nuun to help her begin her journey to motherhood. She could feel the seeds of life come into her. She could feel them attach themselves with love. She could hear the whispers tell her all will soon be well. That she and Ish had done it and she would be with child and without the fear of Hun.

Lut felt the arms of her grandmother reach out and wrap themselves around her. With a deep sigh of hope she snuggled up against Ish and slept as deeply as he did until dawn replaced the night.

CHAPTER 23

Before the moon cycled again, Oohma's behavior changed. Instead of his usual place at Ish's side, he stayed closer to Lut and kept her steadily in his gaze. If anyone other than Ish came near her, Oohma stood alert, showing the whiteness of his teeth.

It was still too early for the first of the signs to show, though she spoke with the spirits. Each night when the moon rose Lut tracked its passage from sliver to full and back again. But the cramps she had expected did not come now even though it was time.

When a second moon passed, a sickness struck Lut in the mornings, weakening her knees and emptying her stomach. She had seen other females do it and tears of joy filled her eyes. She and the old hunter had done it and Hun would never do it or touch her. Not ever.

In the quiet darkness of the hut, on the bearskin Ish had given her, she could feel it when she lay there. Just a whisper still. Still quiet, just beginning to grow. And then she heard something that made her sit up straight. Another whisper. There were two.

Days passed and with it the sickness she felt each morning. Her legs steadied and she stepped outside again. The tall slender grasses growing in wild clumps filled her head with possibilities and questions. She wanted to know.

The sun felt good on her face as she and Oohma climbed the hill and saw it. Lut broke into a run and Oohma paced her as she burst into the grassy field. She dragged her hand over their heavy heads and stripped some of their seeds.

Their scent was pleasant, fresh and green, but too tough to eat. She had learned from other seeds that if she soaked them in water for a day or two, what resisted her teeth would yield to her stone.

She filled a few small sacks with the new grains and returned to their camp. Stepping inside her hut she quickly went to work. Lut filled the hollow of a gourd with water and dumped the seeds inside, then covered them with a small stone. One hand on her growing stomach and one hand on the seed-filled gourd, she waited as patiently as she could.

When the two days finally passed, she drained the seeds and poured them out on her smooth grinding stone. The first of the wet seeds crushed easily, turning to a paste she could mold in her hands.

Lut leaned in close to study it. Its smell was not unpleasant but a small taste of it left her cold. Three days wasted, three days hoping. There was only one thing she had yet to try.

She brushed off the smooth stone and pulled it close to the fire, letting it heat until her hand could not touch it without being burned. She took a fistful of paste and threw it back and forth, then flattened it with her palms.

The stone was making dull, creaking sounds as the heat rose off it. She took the flattened dough and dropped it on. First there was nothing, then a sizzle and then a pop as the center of the dough began to rise and its bottom and edges began to brown. What would happen next she quickly learned as the dough smoked and blackened into a hard, black crisp.

She shook her head up and down, made her uuum sound, then made another round of paste. When the browning started she snatched it off the heat.

An aroma rose off it and filled the tent. The taste of it shocked Lut it was so good. Hungrily, she swallowed it and took another bite and then another and another.

When she finished all she had prepared to bake, she turned to the seeds with a vengeance. The sound of a stone grinding grain could be heard far from her tent as she crushed every seed into powder and added some water.

Making as many patties as the paste would allow, she put them carefully on the hot rock, watching them intently until they were brown.

The aroma drifted out into the campsite air. It drew the tribe like flies as they buzzed around the opening to her tent, questions on their faces and rumblings in their stomachs.

They were not disappointed as she stepped out and broke chunks off the rounds of bread. They sniffed them and clicked and stuffed them in their mouths and clicked again even louder. Their mouths turned upward as she put more into their outstretched hands.

Pointing to the meat sizzling above the fire, she sliced a sliver off and stuffed it inside the hollow of the bread and handed it to Ish.

Ish took one sniff and took it in one bite, the sweet juices running off his lips and down his face. When he finished he quickly gestured for Lut to bring more. That too he greedily devoured.

One by one Lut filled more rounds and passed them around the fire. When all had eaten, the pounding of their feet and spears echoed through the camp. This new wonder Lut had brought them filled every stomach and every eye with admiration.

Lut's name would never be forgotten, not as long as songs were sung and tales were told. Nor would the name of the old hunter who had brought the dogs to them and meat to them.

The eyes of the tribe went back and forth between the old hunter and the medicine woman who was now his mate, and all shared the same thought. What a child they would make.

When all had eaten their fill of the bread and meat, Lut lay down near the fire and called the females to her. There was more to share this night than bread and it would be equally as delicious.

The women placed their hands on the small swell in Lut's breasts and on the bump on her stomach. When Lut smiled and nodded they jumped up to dance.

Soon the men of the tribe understood and banged their spears together with a rhythm that matched the steps of the females. A chant broke out from everyone but Hun.

His face contorted into a snarl as Ish raised his two hands with a look of pride and the tribe responded with yelps of joy.

Once he was safely hidden by the forest and could no longer be seen or heard, Hun let it pour out of him. His own dance was not one of joy, but one of rage. He had had it and he had lost it to an old man well past his prime. The best of the hunt and the choicest of the women would no longer be his. And now she was with child.

He screamed and stomped until he could no more. He fell back against a tree, then sank heavily to the ground. The sharp bark of the oak sliced his tunic into ribbons and dug deep furrows in his back, but all he felt was anger. And the anger brought him a truth.

Ish by himself was nothing. He had not become the tribe's great hunter and leader alone. It was Oohma and without Oohma the old one would be just an old one again.

CHAPTER 24

Oohma could sense the growing strength of Lut's condition and understood she no longer needed his constant attention.

Ish missed Oohma at his side but he welcomed Oohma's protection of Lut. He clapped his hands and the beginnings of a smile softened his face as Oohma ran at him. He had gone from being cast aside and thrown a bone to bewitching the dogs and being able to feed the tribe when no one else could. Now at an age when his own father could no longer walk, he would become a father again.

Ish knelt down on one knee and opened his arms wide. Oohma charged in, rubbing against the insides of Ish's legs and covered his scruffy face with his warm pink tongue.

When Ish stood up again and pointed out to the forest, Oohma's tail swished through the air. He slowed down so Ish could keep up. After a few miles they rounded the low hill that surrounded the meadow and there they were again, just as they had been when he took Lut there. Nine goats, grazing lazily, on the lush grasses of the meadow.

Oohma left Ish standing on the rim of the hill and charged down into the field. The heads of all the goats shot up as they sensed him coming.

They huddled together as they did in times of danger, pressing up against each other so they would look like one giant beast. It was a strategy for survival, not offense.

Oohma did not attack as he and the pack might have. Instead, just as he had done in Ish's vision, he circled the goats again and again, and each time he circled, he pressed them in closer and closer.

Ish watched from the crest of the hill. He still wasn't sure why Oohma was running in circles when he could take any one that he wanted with one lunge.

Oohma smelled Ish's confusion. He stopped circling the goats and trotted back to Ish, panting at his side. Once the goats sensed the danger was over, they moved into the grasses again.

Oohma let them settle. He tore down the hill and circled around them once again, pushing them one way, then turning and pushing them back. When he looked back, Ish was standing, his eye wide open as his vision came to life. Why take one goat when you can take them all?

Ish called Oohma back and retreated up the hill, then down the path toward the campsite. Things were now spinning in his head, making him dizzy and uneasy.

New things were always dangerous things until their uses were known. At the camp Ish would see if Lut could help him use them.

CHAPTER 25

Each time she patted her belly and felt life stir within her, she marveled at the roots and purple flowers Oohma had found for her and at what they had done for Ish.

In her excitement she had forgotten about the other gift Oohma had dug out for her along with the ginseng. The hard seeds with the slender green shoots poking out of them.

But now that her mind was back to her healing potions and caring for the ills and injuries of the tribe, a vision of the sprouting seeds danced in front of her eyes, sending chills up her spine.

She knew just where she put them, in the corner of her tent bathed in the shafts of sunlight that poked in as the sun climbed up. But whether they were still green and growing or dead and crumbled, that she did not know.

They were where she thought they would be, in a leather sack, sitting in a hollowed gourd of water. She removed the sack and let the dirty water drip onto the ground. An earthy, loamy scent drifted up and surrounded her.

Lut knelt down and let the seeds spill out of the sack. A web grew out of them woven of tender, hair-like roots. When the first one tumbled out free, she bit off the shoot. It tasted fresh and lively, but that was not what put that look on her face. She felt her ears start buzzing and her legs go unsteady. As she slid to the ground what it meant washed over her, bringing both her hands to her stomach to feel the lives inside her.

Just as she was her babies' mother, the seeds were the plants' mothers. And just as she could take her babies anywhere she wanted and watch them grow, could she not do the same with the seeds? Put them where she wanted and watch them grow?

Her digging stick was out of the corner of her tent in a second. She ran to a sunny secret spot in the forest behind it and began to dig.

When a shallow furrow was scraped out, Lut sprinkled in the seeds and brushed the dirt back on top of them. She poured a trickle of water over each until the earth was wet but still firm. Now all she could do was wait.

It took two long weeks of sun for it to happen. But finally a small spot of earth yielded to a persistent shoot, with others just like it beginning to show their heads.

Lut could hardly contain her excitement when she saw the first of the shoots poke out of the dirt. But knew she had to until she was sure of what she had and how to use it.

That night at the fire, after the tribe had once again eaten well, Lut raised her staff and issued a warning in ways they could understand.

She had found a place in the forest and would tell them where. *Until then they were to go nowhere near it, touch nothing, pick no green thing anywhere near it.*

The tribe looked puzzled as she clicked out her warning, but no one thought to question the words of the medicine woman.

Each morning when the sky grew light, Lut slipped out of the tent and rushed to see what the long night had brought.

Using a small twig, she measured the shoots' progress and clicked a happy sound as it continued to grow taller.

After a few weeks it stopped at her knee and a cluster of small hard seeds began to crown its head. Once again the happy sound bounced off her lips. The wild grains she had gathered and put in the ground had become tame and were starting to bloom.

No more would she and the others of the tribe have to trudge miles to find and gather these grains. No more would they head out not knowing if they would return.

When she lay quietly, feeling the movement in her belly in the stillness of the night, she knew why she had lived. Why the trees had spoken to her. Why the spirits had sent Ish and the tribe, the dogs and the secrets of the seeds.

Each time she closed her eyes she could see fields with grains of grass growing without limits. Food without shortage, the pangs of hunger in the tribe's stomachs a thing of the past.

Tears of joy striped her glowing face. She knew something every mother who had ever lived could appreciate and share. Her babies would be born in a different world, one with far less struggle, one with far more food. What better gift could a mother give her children?

She could feel the pride swell along with her belly. What would her grandmother Nuun think of the dull-faced girl now, whose only strengths had been her legs?

CHAPTER **26**

Ish returned to the campsite, his head spinning from what Oohma had shown him. There was an answer but he was not yet sure of the question. It would take Lut to help him make sense of it and how it could be used.

The tribesmen saw him enter the camp and moved to greet him but he raised his hand to push them back. It was only Lut he wanted to see now. The tribe would have to wait.

Lut could see the frustration on his face when he entered their tent. She had seen that look before and knew she must calm him first. Placing her hands on his shoulders, she held him in her soothing eyes.

Ish shook his right arm in the air, turning it in circles and then pointing at Oohma. He waited, but Lut did nothing but furrow her brow. He picked up a stick and dropped to his knees and drew stick figures of goats. Then he waved his arm around and pointed at Oohma. It did no good. Lut did not yet understand.

In frustration he jumped up and pointed back at Oohma, then at himself and began to run in circles. The look on Lut's face changed as the picture became clear. Oohma and the pack could circle the goats and keep them still. But then what? The pack could not circle forever.

Still, if the dogs could control and move them, just like putting the seeds where she wanted, putting the goats where she wanted made the earth stand still. A look flashed across her face and she jumped up and ran outside, taking her sharp stone knife and Ish with her.

Ish watched her slash a few branches and drop them end to end in a small circle on the ground. Inside it she put a few small stones. Ish pounded one leg on the ground and the corners of his lips turned up. Just as branches laid tightly together could keep out the sun, branches laid end to end in a circle could keep in the flock.

Lut turned to Ish and Ish took her by the shoulders and both roared until tears streamed down their faces. Just as she always did, Lut had the answer.

Ish was outside gathering the males of the tribe in seconds, Lut right behind him. With signs and gestures and clicks and whistles, he showed them what to do. Hack down enough bushy branches with their sharp stone axes and place them in a wide circle in the grassy field next to their camp. When he knew they understood, he set off with Oohma at his side.

That night Ish did not return. But when morning came clouds of dust, the sharp scent of game and the bleating of goats filled the air above the camp trail.

The hunters acted quickly, leaping for their spears, ready for a kill. But Lut rushed out in front of them making the signal to stand and wait.

Tension crackled through the air as they stood there. Why were they not racing to the kill?

Ish held them back with his raised hand as the pack continued running in circles, keeping the flock of goats under control.

Ish ran for the circle and split it open, towing a large branch aside to let the flock, driven by the pack, inside. A whistling sound brought the pack out again and Ish pulled the branch back into place, leaving the goats huddled together in the corral.

For hours he stood there, Oohma at his side, as all the tribesmen brought their mates and their young to see the wonder of the goats inside the circle.

These were theirs now. They would no longer have to go out and find them. They were just where they put them, feeding on the tender green grass.

CHAPTER 27

Ish could not get over the thrill of watching the goats calmly graze. Oohma followed him to the corral everyday, watching Ish watch them to learn their habits and their ways. Once the food they were given each day overcame their initial panic, the goats became docile, allowing Oohma, Ish and Lut to come close and walk among them.

Two of the female goats had given birth and their kids nursed at their sagging udders. Ish watched the she-goats' white milk be hungrily taken by their newborn kids. When the kids finished nursing and pulled away, often the milk continued to flow.

Ish stepped up slowly, careful not to startle one and make her run away. When he was next to her, he took his hand and patted the goat's head, scratching his rough fingers between the goat's ears. He could feel the tension leave the goat's body. As he reached down a small stream of warm milk puddled in his hand.

Licking his lip he squeezed the goat's udder again and once again his hand filled with white. His mouth bent upward as he looked them over. Four she-goats would have enough milk for all the tribe.

Before Ish heard it Oohma was already at his side, flying as fast as his legs would let him. Ish soon heard why. The first screams of birth wailed out.

When he reached the front of the tent, he dared not go in. The mysteries of birth were woman's work, something no man could help with or understand. All he could do was walk to one end of the camp then walk back again to the other.

Every time Lut screamed out, it was like a spear piercing his chest. Her young body was strong. But it could barely manage the pain of a baby forcing its way out, much less two. After what seemed like hours, Lut's cries stopped and Ish froze solid. At least when she was screaming Ish knew she was alive.

But his fears ended when the new sounds began. They were the first calls to the world of a newborn being born. And minutes later there was a second.

Once the bleeding stopped, two of the midwives struggled to help Lut stand. She walked outside of the hut and one of the midwives followed her, holding a baby, pink and bawling in her arms. Gently she handed it to Lut and Lut, beaming, held it high above her.

An explosion of joy filled the campsite. The tribesmen banged their hands against their chests, screaming out over and over. And the females spun into ecstasy, shrieking as they did.

But a moment later every sound, every breath, every heart stopped as a second midwife stepped out of the tent with a second baby in her arms and held him out for Ish.

A look no one had ever seen crossed Ish's face as he took his baby boy and lifted him high up over his head. He turned him so that all could see he held his son. The silence ended and the chanting began.

"Lut. Ish. Lut. Ish." One by one they picked it up and then they picked up Ish and put him on their shoulders and raced around the campsite yelping his name, the dogs right behind them barking as loud.

That night at the fire, Moc, a short hunter with dark piercing eyes brought something new to the fire, as he often did. Weeks before he had stretched a length of deerskin over a hollowed stump to dry out, but he had forgotten it. When he returned to get it, it had shrunk so tightly around the stump he could not get it off.

Frustration filled his face at the waste of a precious skin. He raised his hand in ire and struck the center of the taut skin, hoping it would free. Instead it snapped back at him with a deep husky sound. He leaped back in fear. A voice that boomed that loud, that low, usually lived inside a powerful body.

Was this some kind of creature he had never seen before? Was this a sound of warning like the rattle of a snake? He crouched down on one knee, waiting for what would happen next. But nothing did. Just the sound of the drum echoing up into the air each time his hand pounded down on it.

Leaning in close to the flames, Moc placed the drum between his strong thighs. No one seemed to notice until he brought his hand down and began to tap out a sound and then another and another. And then they all noticed as a rhythm filled them like a second heartbeat, making them stand and jump.

The males picked up their spears and began to circle the fire, hopping and leaping as they did, their legs moving to the beat.

Soon the females and their babies joined, increasing their speed with every turn until they had spun themselves into exhaustion and fell back down.

As they danced they sang songs. Songs in praise of Lut and the miracle of her two births. Songs in praise of Ish who had conquered the dogs and of his endless powers as a hunter and a man. Songs of Oohma and the pack that now lived among them and filled the corral with goats and their bellies with meat.

As the drumming increased their voices rose until no other sound was heard anywhere in the night.

But of Hun there were no songs. No words of praise of his skills as a hunter or of the sharp edges he could chip from dull stones. When none looked his way he turned from the fire and escaped deep into the forest where no one could hear him. He pounded on the rough bark of a fallen tree until his hands were bloody and he was out of breath from screaming oaths and curses.

Now each day that Hun lived Ish bettered him. Each day the tribe let him know he was no longer their leader but just one of them. And each day Hun swore an oath: That day would soon end.

CHAPTER **28**

On the morning after the twins arrived, Ish took one baby in each arm and tugged them tight against the morning chill, leaving the camp and the tribe behind him. Oohma stayed close to him as he picked his way up a rocky path and out toward the wide valley below. When they reached it, the sun had yet to rise high enough and throw off its blanket of mist. Ish would have to wait.

All that had happened could not have just happened. The twins had to be a gift of the gods, just as Oohma and the pack had been, just as Lut and all her secrets and whispers had been. And if that were so, something of equal value must be given in return. It was the rule all knew and lived by.

Ish laid the babies at his feet on a soft patch of grass and sat patiently, waiting for the first crack of sun to show its face over the mountain rim.

Slowly the sun climbed up his body. When it reached his head he stood up and reached back down for the babies and slowly lifted them to his chest.

He looked at the round faces of the babies still asleep in his arms and listened to their gentle breathing as he walked to the edge of the cliff. Lifting them high above him, he waited for the wind to call out to him to tell him what it wanted. Was it the girl or the boy?

A powerful gust slammed into him as he stood there, pushing him back off the edge and making him huddle against the rocks. Just as suddenly the wind calmed, then stopped.

Ish stumbled and fell to his knees and tears filled his eyes as he crouched there trembling. The winds had spoken. They did not want his babies.

He took the other tribute he had brought with him, the spear he had fashioned to honor his own father and treasured above all else. This time the winds grew gentle when he stepped to the edge of the rim again. He drew back his arm and threw it with all the strength he had.

Welcomed by the wind it sailed out of sight into the mist below. Bursts of warmth radiated through his chest as he chanted to the spirits, the sound of his own voice catching in his throat. He reached out and stroked the soft hair on both babies' heads and snuggled them tightly to his heaving chest.

Oohma could feel the emotions surge through Ish and he leaned his body against Ish's bent legs, gently licking his hands and arms. Drawing in a deep breath, Ish reached over and patted Oohma's head. Oohma bent down and licked each baby's head and face before they set back for camp.

The tribeswomen were pacing nervously, their eyes on the hill, when Ish and Oohma came down it. Low whistles of relief jumped out of them when they saw both babies in his arms and their worst fears were put to rest.

They ran up to take the babies from him but Ish pushed them back. Raising the boy to his shoulder he sung out, "Isha. Isha. Isha," over and over and the tribe screamed back the name.

Then he looked over at Lut and she came close as he handed her the baby girl and yelled, "Lutta, Lutta, Lutta." Her face beamed as the tribe burst into whoops and yells.

CHAPTER 29

Moons had gone from slice to circle since Lut visited the small patch of grasses she had planted with a hope and a sharp stick. The seeds that had grown inside of her had taken all her thoughts, all her strength and all her energy. But now that the twins had survived their birth and were growing quickly, their daily care shifted away from only Lut to all of the women of the tribe.

Mating, among the males and females, just happened. All were the tribe and all were each other's. Families had not yet begun. But as more and more tents rose up, what was once communal was becoming individual, bringing with it a new idea, yours and mine.

Lut set off early, taking Oohma with her. Leaving the twins behind with the other tribeswomen, she set out for the little patch she had left so long unattended.

The days had been rainy and warm, filling the landscape with green growing plants all around her. Oohma stayed close, alert to any sights or scents. His hair bristled as they rounded a small hill and a scream jumped out of Lut that made the birds go silent.

Spinning quickly he bared his teeth and crouched into a defensive position. But there were only Lut's arms spread wide like wings flying through the field of waving grasses. What was dirt just months before was now tall and green and dancing in the wind.

She fell to her knees and watched the blades shake, dropping a few seeds each time they did. Seeing them blow along the ground until they caught some dirt, she saw how the patch had spread so far. She wanted to dance but she knew it was too soon.

They looked the same, but would they crush to powder and mix with water and become a paste as the first seeds had? Would they brown on the cooking stone and make stomachs roar?

Grasses fell as her blade slashed through them, first from one part of the field and then from others. When her arms could hold no more, she ran for her crushing stone, her heart filled with hope.

Would it happen again? Would the powdered seeds drink in the water and become what she now called dah? She had to wait and soak them first. The time would drag like stone.

When two days had passed she drained them and stoked the ashes in her small fire. Once her spit on the stone began to sizzle, she molded the paste into palm-sized rounds and dropped them on the hot stone.

In minutes the aroma of baking bread began to fill the air and every one in the camp with hunger.

They crowded outside Lut's tent waiting for her to come out. A murmur of joy passed through them as she filled their hands with bread.

With the last crumb eaten the stomping began. The women jumped up on their feet and broke into a dance. They nodded to Lut as they spun by her, chanting, "Lut. Lut. Lut."

They rang out over and over, hailing her *as the maker of twin babies. As the maker of bread. As the maker of miracles.*

The praise rained down on her until she would hear no more and went inside again, but not to rest or hide her crimson cheeks. She steadied herself as she had taught herself to let the vision come. The mists cleared and a clearing bathed by the sun stood out where thick forest now stood.

A small leathered figure drifted out of the shadows at her. The face had changed, now gentler, and the once cloudy eyes beamed bright. But Lut knew her well.

The ancient hand reached out and touched Lut's face. Its loving warmth set her cheeks aglow. A moment passed and then another until Lut knew what to do.

The howls and barks of the pack returning to camp snapped her out of her trance. She was outside in seconds and the men knew when they saw her face they would get no rest. The tree-filled space between the campsite and the corral was going to become a field.

Everyone went to their tents to sleep knowing the next days and nights would be long. Keeping the fires burning hot enough to burn the green trees in the field would be hard, but nothing like hacking at them with axes of stone. The tribesmen shook their heads as they left the fire. How did Lut know what she knew?

CHAPTER 30

When morning came the tribe came out and piled dried grasses around the trees. And on their trunks they rubbed a coating of animal fat they used to keep their torches burning.

One tree at a time so the entire forest would not explode, they kept the flames going until the charred trunks could be pushed over to the ground.

The tribesmen worked till their hands blistered and bled. But not Hun's. He had kept far away.

The sky was darkening when he returned to the camp and Lut was standing outside of her hut. Hun's mouth went wet and his pace increased as a jolt of energy surged through him.

She heard his steps gaining on her and stepped back, putting some space between them again. He stopped for a beat to watch her take a strip of white bark in her hand and wave it in his face.

Hun grabbed it from her and studied it briefly as his blood cooled. Then his eyes narrowed and his brow furrowed. Lut tilted her face up, pointing her chin at the bark. *Look at it*, she gestured.

The simple drawing looked like a spear, but the shaft was much thicker and the stone tip attached to its end much larger and sturdier.

The question didn't leave Hun's face. So Lut lifted her arms and brought them down with a chopping motion, kicking at the dirt with the heel of her foot.

Hun let out a deep grunt and shook his head, finally understanding. He pointed at the interior of his hut, where his chipping tools were. He motioned for Lut to follow him in.

Oohma jumped up as the tent flap closed behind Lut. When he could no longer see her he raced over and paced nervously around it. His ears perked, alert to any sound, any sign of danger.

Hun reeked of predator. Oohma could sense it the first moment he saw him. He knew never to trust Hun. Not when Hun was near Ish and especially not when Hun was near Lut or the babies.

Hun closed the flap tighter and turned to Lut, moving in too close. She pushed him back with all her strength, but Hun's strength was so much greater.

Before the dogs and before the tents he took any female he wanted with no complaints or refusals. Why was it different now? Was the tribe led by a man or a dog?

Lut spun on one foot to leave but Hun grabbed her, pulling her back and locking her to him. With his massive arms he pushed her to the ground. She let out a startled cry as she fell.

Oohma was in the air before Lut's cry ended. Crashing through the opening of the tent, he flew into Hun in full gallop, knocking him through the skins at the back.

Oohma grabbed Lut and pulled her outside before the bones of the tent crashed down. When he was sure Lut was safe, he turned back to Hun.

His nails extended, his teeth bared, he came at Hun ready to kill. The intensity of his growls shook Oohma's whole body as he stood over Hun, hatred dripping from his open mouth all over Hun's face.

He could have taken Hun in a moment, but he did not. Taking one of your own pack and tribe was not to be taken lightly. Both knew this was a warning. Both knew there would not be another.

The tribe gathered that night at the fire, but not to eat. Lut stood near Ish at the head of the fire without saying a word and she let the silence build. Even the pack slunk away to the edges of the camp, knowing something was coming and it was not going to be good.

Every head turned toward Lut as she pointed a shaking finger at Hun and told the tribe her story. Had it been any other female, Hun's actions would be nothing, but not the medicine woman, not the leader's woman. That could not be allowed.

Ish moved in closer to Lut as she spoke. Hun sat at the other end of the fire alone. The flames pointed out the differences in their faces. Hun, jaw locked, chin jutted, eyes dead like blackened coals. Ish in control of his power, strangely calm, not angry, but hard.

The pack, sensing the heaviness of the moment, paced back and forth at the edges. None had taken to Hun. Not when his fist or his foot came at them so often.

Ish let the moment build as he lifted his arm and pointed his finger, first at Hun and then at the forest.

A murmur of shock rippled through the tribe. They had lost members to many things before, deaths of all kinds, but never this kind of loss.

Hun jumped up defiantly and lunged for the closest spear, but all the men of the tribe were on their feet just as quickly, taking a defensive position around Ish and Lut.

If any had felt any sorrow for Hun, it disappeared now. Hun was no longer part of them and now he, like any other stranger, was an enemy in competition for what the earth had to offer.

Oohma watched Hun storm from the fire and stuff his few belongings into his leather pouch, his flint chipping tools, an extra skin used to cover himself and a small stone knife. Taking his two spears, one in either hand, Hun turned his back on the tribe as they had on him and walked defiantly away.

The tribesmen stood mute at the edge of the clearing, watching Hun disappear into the thick forest, some still torn by what they were seeing.

Yes, Hun was more brutal than any of them. More willing to lash out at any of them with little reason, but still he had been one of them, and never had any of them, in memory or in legend, been driven away.

They stood there until Hun's screams could no longer be heard, then they turned for the fire and sat down in silence. Ish let them brood for a while as he drilled into them with his one good eye and they looked away.

No one challenged Ish or spoke out on Hun's behalf. Their bellies were too full. For the first time, they had a place to sleep, a tent of their own that was warm and dry and protectors much more alert to danger and much better at the hunt than they were. And that was because of Ish.

Oohma watched Hun disappear into the trees, but he knew he had not seen the last of him. With his tail tucked tightly underneath him, Oohma followed Ish back to the fire. Ish reached over for him and pulled him closer, stroking his coat gently, but Oohma would not quiet. Hun was gone but not his threat.

Each morning Lut visited the new field the men had cleared, to see what the night had brought. Dropping on her knees, she put her ear down and listened. They were low and they were far away still, but whispers of life were beginning to echo through the dirt and into her.

The males passed her kneeling in her field as they went off to hunt. They shook their heads knowing that the medicine woman was rarely wrong. Still, all their work, all the sweat and blood from swollen hands and torn-up knees and nothing.

When the moon came full circle again, nothing became something. Tiny puffs of green began to poke through the dark soil, exactly where Lut had put the hard black seeds, in neat straight rows she knew were hers.

The moment she saw them her eyes filled with tears. She walked quickly but unsteadily to her tent. Ish was still sleeping on his mat when she shook him awake.

He reached for his spear in panic, an uncertain look on his face, but Lut reached out to calm him. Pushing his spear back down, she pulled the old man to his feet and began pulling him by his hand along the trail to the field.

When she reached the place where plants had begun to sprout, she stopped and pointed down. It took a moment for Ish to understand what he was being shown, but soon his lip began to quiver and a faraway look crossed his face.

He brushed his hand over the small green growths and bent down to sniff their fresh scent. When Ish reached out to pick one, Lut pushed his hand away. She then slowly raised her hands up to show him why. He knew not to touch them now. They had only just begun to grow.

Taking a few steps back, he found Lut's eyes again. He stood there for a moment, wonder sweeping through his ancient body, just as it had when the winds took his spear and not his babies. Just as it had when Oohma came up beside him and put his head on his old leg.

The light around Lut's face shimmered, split into shards of color by the wetness of his eye. This girl, whose face was once dull, whose only value had been the strength of her legs, who had endured the sneers and jabs of the tribe and Nuun, especially Nuun, her wise but harsh grandmother, was now the maker of miracles, the queen of all the females of the tribe. No one could surpass her. No one ever would. And she was his, not Hun's.

Together they walked back to their tent, Lut's hand resting lightly on Oohma's head. Ish looked down and moved his hand on top of hers. She did not take it away. Instead she reached for his and squeezed it tightly.

A look crossed her face, bending her thick lips into an upturned curve. From the corner of her eye, she watched his crooked walk and the wind blowing the few gray hairs on his head. She made a soft haha that Ish could not hear. That was good. It was meant for her and no one else, especially Ish. She had been given the oldest tree in the forest and he was still giving the most fruit.

CHAPTER 32

Many moons had passed and Hun had endured. Kept alive by his skills with his spear, a nose that could find tubers and an anger that would not leave him.

The air had changed. Hun sensed a tang in his nose and a sharp taste in the back of his throat. And a dampness surrounded him each day. So different than the dryness he was used to.

All was new to him. The tribe had lived and trekked inland all their lives, not even aware that land could end.

When his senses adjusted, something far more familiar drifted up at him. It was the smell of others not so different than himself.

After months of being alone and apart, Hun felt a wave of relief. But the wave soon gave way to fear. Now that he had scented them, he had no sense of them. Who were they? What were they? Would they welcome him or hunt him down? Deep inside him he knew it made no difference. He could no longer live on his own. Either could bring him death.

Hun found a deep depression in a wall of rock and pressed himself into its darkness. A small crack above his head let in some fingers of light. Standing on his toes, he pulled himself up to look out, but it did no good. He could smell them. He could hear them. But he could see nothing but trees and sky and stone.

The sharp snap of a branch below him, then a series of clicks and whistles, harsh and threatening, filled the air. Hun could not understand the meaning, but he understood the anger in the sharpness of its tone.

He looked out again, straining his eyes and shielding them with his hand. But no matter how intently he looked there was still nothing to see, just a broad open plain with a stand of trees. But suddenly the stand of trees stopped standing and started walking.

Hun's heart jumped and he jumped back into the safety of the rocks. He needed to think for a moment to let it all sink in. He had lived in forests all his life surrounded by trees that grew tall and thick, trees that bore sweet and luscious fruit. Trees whose leaves changed colors with the seasons. But never trees that walked.

He wanted to stay hidden, but he could not stay still. He crawled out of his hiding place, staying low to the ground. Whatever it was, it was something he had never seen before and that meant he had to know it.

A vision of Lut's knowing face came to him, along with a wish that she were with him. If anyone would know what it was and what to do, it would be Lut.

Quietly, Hun crawled through the forest cover until he was close enough to a tree to realize that the tree wasn't a tree, but a man, cleverly covered with different shades of mud to look like a tree trunk. Even his wrists and legs were covered with bundles of leaves and twigs.

Hun's eyes narrowed as the tree took a few slow steps, then stopped and stood perfectly still, arms spread out, palms open wide. It took a while, but Hun understood as the flapping of wings stirred the air above the tree man. A large black bird was circling slowly. After a few cautious turns it landed on an outstretched arm.

The tree man let the bird settle. Let it pace up and down searching for insects. With all the bird's attention on its hunt, a hand shot out and snapped its neck. Hun grunted approvingly to himself as he took in the trees' craft.

His eyes scanned their bodies from head to toe, looking for places they might be hiding their weapons but there were none to see. All they had was mud. They had no spears, no stone axes or sharp obsidian blades. That made his breath come easier. He had them all.

CHAPTER **33**

Once the trees had made their kills, they piled the fallen birds onto a sheet of woven palm. A few quick turns of a length of vine closed it at the top and they prepared themselves for the most dangerous part of the hunt. Getting back alive.

The predators that roamed the forest, lions, saber-tooth tigers, boars and hyenas, might be fooled by their treelike look but not by the scent of the fresh kill they were dragging behind them.

Hun watched them with unwavering eyes until a low growl boomed out from the bush behind him. It grew louder as it closed in on him. Hun knew what it was.

He squatted low before springing up to grab the thick branch of a giant oak tree, then pulled himself up to hide.

A low whistle blew out of him as a dark shadow set loose by the setting sun moved under him. He knew its sound, its screeching cackle, its rancid scent. He had seen its pack tear through the muscular body of a lion in seconds. The hyena stalked in, too riveted on the dead birds on the mat to see him in the tree, as always preferring to scavenge than hunt.

Once it moved past him, Hun swung down to see what would happen next. He knew what the hyena could do, but what the tree men would do, he could only watch and see.

The hyena moved in closer, stalking low to the ground and except by him, unseen and unheard. Hun could feel his grip instinctively tighten around his spear and his muscles grow taut as he moved in closer to watch.

The hyena picked up speed now that his targets were in sight. Hun could see its strategy. Leap at the tree, drive them back, steal their prey, turn and run away. As he knelt down to watch, the hyena sprang into the air.

He knew he shouldn't, but he could not help himself. Every instinct, every gene in his body was screaming in his ears like his father had done. Hun had a split second to choose. *Run at or run from. To hesitate is to die.*

His feet hit the ground, his spear in his left hand, a knife in his right. He could not tell who was more startled, the hyena or the tree men, as he flew down at them.

The hyena retreated a few steps, then stopped and made his stand. It stood just long enough for Hun to take aim and throw his spear. Whistling through the air, it hit with a thud, then plunged deep into the hyena, pinning it howling to the ground.

Hun was over it in a few long strides. Putting one powerful leg on the hyena's quivering body, he yanked the spear back out with a savage twist.

Not a sound cut through the air. Not from the wind or the brush, not from the tree people or Hun. They stood and stared at each other, then down at the dead hyena, then back at each other again.

Had they and their prey just been saved by this stranger? Was he another predator, coming at them to kill?

When the moment of shock ended, the trees stepped out and circled Hun, clicking and grunting and nodding at him and each other as they did.

Hun let them study him, let them touch his spears and his knives and stroke the skins he was wearing, all from ferocious animals they knew well. The tree that seemed to be their leader came close and sniffed Hun up and down, front and back.

When Hun offered no resistance and made no sudden moves, the leader motioned for the trees. They dragged the hyena's body and put it on the mat next to the birds. Then he turned to Hun, stripping the leaves from his wrists and ankles and motioning for Hun to follow.

CHAPTER 34

Squeals of happy chattering filled the fields as the twins ran and played. Seasons had come and gone and their heads already showed above the blades of grain.

Under the watchful eye of Lut and the special foods she made them, they had grown quickly. And under the watchful eye of Oohma, no threat came near them. Still Oohma watched in wonder at how long Lut's pups remained pups, still needing care when any of his pack would already be on their own.

But there was no denying that the things the twins had already learned to do, none of the pack would ever be able to do.

Already they could lift and carry, throw and chase and make the clicking sounds and balance on their two back paws while they climbed and ran. But of all the things they could do, none made Oohma feel the way their little paws did wrapped around his neck and their small, warm faces pressed into his thick, soft coat.

Love, unlike fear and hunger, was as new to the pack as the tribe was. Something they had never known before, or ever felt. Not at their mother's breast, not snuggled next to their brothers and sisters sharing their mother's warmth, not joining the hunt with the others of the pack.

But now, each time a hand found their heads or touched their furry bodies, each time they were thrown a meaty bone or walked alongside one of the tribe or slept near them, the feeling grew and filled them.

Isha, the boy, already had the instincts of a hunter. Oohma could see that grow each day, in the way he ran along the ground grabbing at bugs, in the way his eyes roamed the world around him, taking it in the way a hunter's should. Oohma's love for him grew every day seeing that he would be everything his father Ish was and more.

Unlike the other fathers, who ignored their children until they had grown enough to help and hunt, Ish gave his time to the little boy, showing him what he would need to survive in the world and survive as leader of the tribe. Showing him how to hunt and chip, snare and trap, but more than that, Ish taught him the thing every leader must know. How to listen before he made a decision.

The little girl, Lutta, was like dry earth, soaking in everything she watched Lut do. When Lut pointed at something, Lutta could get it, then come sit at Lut's knee and watch her blend it into a drink Lut tried on herself first, then on Ish, if she could make him, which she could not always do.

More than once, Ish spit one of Lut's potions across the floor and sent a dagger at her with his one good eye. When he did, Lut would point at the twins and the sacks of goat weed and the ginseng potion until Ish made a sour face, gave in, and drank some more.

CHAPTER 35

The sound of tree limbs snapping and thunder clapping kept the tribe warm and dry inside their tents. Since the pack had come to them, there was always meat to eat, so they could wait for the storm to pass.

But Baba could not. The visions that had grown inside him were desperate to be free. He wrapped an oiled deer skin over his head and around his pots of red ochre and charcoal black. Lightening etched the sky as he was swallowed up by the darkness.

Oohma followed close behind and shook himself dry as he moved into the shadows. What magic Baba's hands would bring alive this day, Oohma was eager to see.

Baba went to work placing the paints next to the wall and his red-tipped sticks at his feet. He took a small bundle of dried grass from a niche in the cave wall and bent over it with his flint.

It took three strikes for a spark to jump out and find the dried grass, and a moment more for a small spark to become a flame. Baba used it to light a second one close by and then the tip of a fat-soaked torch. He sat down with a heavy sigh, picking his visions apart so he could lay them down with purpose.

Under the flickering light the limestone walls flowed like a rushing river. The swells and hollows seemed to move under his torch. He lifted it up and down and then moved it side to side to see how he could use the shadows to make his drawings move.

Each time he stepped back, Oohma stood up, and each time he moved in, Oohma sat down again. Over and over Baba attacked, then retreated, sometimes shaking his head side to side and sometimes up and down.

A low growl shook Oohma as the play of light and shadows found a saber-tooth tiger and made it move. Baba's swift strokes bent the tiger's body around a bulge in the wall, so it looked back over its shoulder as it ran, its nostrils flaring. If he didn't know better, Oohma would have jumped up to save himself and Baba from the tiger's jaws.

As Baba left behind more red lines, what they were began to make sense. Like the visions in his sleep that made him whimper and move his paws, the animals Baba was putting on the walls were real, but only in their world on the cave wall and on the tents where Baba made them live.

He kept at it for hours, into the paint pot, then back to the wall, until the fat-soaked torch burned out along with his energy.

Exhausted, he walked back to the campsite. He needed some meat. He needed some sleep. There was paint to make and sticks to cut and hours of drawing to do in the morning.

The females screamed and ran to help him when Baba stepped into the light of the fire. A collective sigh of relief escaped their lips when they realized the red dripping off his hands and body was paint and not blood.

The men at the fire spread wide to open a place for Baba and he joined them with a heavy sigh. He held out his hand and one of the females filled it with a wide leaf.

Baba tore into the hunks of meat with the last of his strength, and when he finished he licked the leaf clean and drank a full measure of water.

Like Lut, he was provided for, even though he did not hunt. The tribe's strong arms would take down the animals, while Baba's magic fingers would keep their spirits close forever on the cave wall.

CHAPTER 36

Baba's tired, red eyes opened slowly and he felt his shoulders scream as he moved his arms around him and walked to the fire. For days, for weeks and months he had climbed all over the walls, reaching up, reaching out, reaching back, reaching his red-tipped stick into the pot of paint, over and over again, then stepping back to see if the lines had listened to what his heart had said.

A yelp flew out of him into the inky darkness as he turned the pot upside down and shook it close to his flaming torch. Except for a few red spots, there was nothing left to use. What he needed would take some searching and that would take some time.

A towering rock, set back from the cave, had the telltale sign he was looking for, a rusty ribbon of red, trickling down the rough stone. His hand reached up and felt a clump of red iron oxide poking out of it, close enough to get.

He dragged over a rock he could stand on and reached up to pry it out with his blade. When he had it free, he took it down and crushed it into a fine powder, with a hard grind of his foot. Before the breeze could take it, he brushed the red powder into his palm and carefully poured it into the paint pot.

What came next was easier to find. Thickets of raspberry bushes grew in the brush all around them. A sour look painted his face as his eyes ran over them. They were covered with thorns, but except for a few white and green ones they were empty of red, ripe berries.

Baba pulled Oohma closer as he walked farther into the thick bushes. There were more Baba could see at the edge of a swampy bog, covered with slimy green water.

He took a breath and put his foot into the water, but took it out even quicker as a ripple crossed it. Something he couldn't see moved beneath its murky surface.

He let out a sigh of relief when he saw dark circles of red on the ground that must have fallen off, ripe and full of juice. It looked like there were enough of them to make into the paint he needed.

The moment his arms moved at them, the red circles moved back, coiling their bodies, baring their fangs. Oohma moved just as quickly, barking sharply as he jumped, knocking Baba's hand away as the startled vipers slithered away, back into the brush.

Baba brushed the mud from his arms and reached out to take Oohma and squeeze him tight. He stroked him and turned back for the cave. He knew where some other raspberries might be and he turned for them, making sure Oohma turned with him.

There were just enough when he found them. He took two fists full. Now he needed some blood and his urine to fix the ingredients so his marks would last, not fade out and die.

He bit down on his lip as he held out his wrist. He squinted his eyes tight and pulled his knife across it and let the trickle of blood drip into the paint pot at his feet.

Oohma was on his paws, his head tilting back and forth as he watched Baba feed the paint his blood. Now Oohma knew Baba's magic. It was his blood, not just his hands, that gave the paintings life.

CHAPTER 37

Hun had never forgotten the first thing his father had taught him when he was old enough to listen. A hunter needs to know everything around him if he wants to stay alive.

As he walked behind them, his eyes swept the forest. Every rock, every bush, every tree, those he knew and those he didn't he studied carefully, fixing their looks and their locations as he walked.

The day would come, he knew it, when it would be time to leave. It was carved into the hard lines of his face and the set of his cold, tight lips.

The trail they followed was wide, the brush alongside it crudely snapped, not having been smoothly sliced by a blade. The same strange look crossed Hun's face as it had when the hyena threatened. Once again his head shook as he walked behind them. No weapons. No tools, just mud and patience and their bare hands.

He'd been chipping blades so long, as his grandfather had done before him and all his line before that. Hun could not remember when he hadn't. But these trees either had no use for blades or did not know how to make them. And that made them more prey than hunters.

He grunted softly and shook his head slowly as the tension that had built up inside of him began to fade away. Any tribe, anyone, could be an enemy to fear, but one man with a knife and a spear was worth 20 without.

After miles of trudging, they suddenly reached a crude clearing. He had not smelled any cooking fires. One quick look told him why.

There were none. No fire pits, no ashes anywhere. And their camp was nothing. Little more than a crudely cleared opening and a few ribs of thin branches covered over with leaves.

A buzz flew through the camp when they saw him. The new tribe circled and stared at him. He stood stone still and let them. What could they do that he could not undo with a jab of his knife and his spear?

Hun looked around more closely this time, but nothing changed. Not only were there no fires, there were no tools or weapons of any kind and no animal skins pegged out to dry.

The few signs of the tribe's successful hunting other than the birds were the strange bones of fish, larger than any Hun had known in the streams and rivers, bleached white on the ground. And near them, a mound of unknown shells that had been pried open. They were things he had never seen before that must have come from a place of mystery.

The small coverings the females wore were not soft skins, but harsh mats woven from palm fronds. Without weapons and the skills to use them, there was no chance of them taking prey and no way to scavenge one away from other predators with more strength and speed and skills.

They had not mastered much, but Hun could see that they were masters of disguise. His spears and their invisibility could make him more dangerous than he had ever been.

The women of the new tribe stayed a safe distance back, their noses ridging as they drew in Hun's unfamiliar smell.

One, a bent and shrunken hag with a toothless face and bands of woven leaves in her thin gray hair, stepped up and hesitated before she reached out to touch the lion skin Hun wore, as though the lion still might be inside it, ready to leap out at her.

When she was sure it was just a skin, she lifted it and made a low click. The old woman locked Hun in her gaze as she reached for the leather sheaf at his waist. When he didn't strike her down, she pulled his knife out of it.

She ran her finger along the sharp blade and yelped when she pulled it back, blood spouting from her finger and running down her arm.

When she made the bleeding stop, she stepped close to Hun once more and took his spear and jammed it into the ground, nodding toward Hun with a question on her brow.

Hun made a sharp sound and shook his head from side to side, then took the spear back from her and pointed at a tree just behind her. He steadied himself for a second, then let his spear fly.

The tribe sucked in loud breaths as Hun's spear sliced through the air and bit deeply into the trunk of a tree.

Every eye turned to the old woman to see what she was thinking, but all they could see was confusion on her leathered face.

One of the tree men took the old woman's arm and tugged her to the palm mat where the hyena lay dead among the birds. He pointed at the hyena, then at Hun and made a motion of throwing the spear into the tree. A torrent of sharp clicking sounds and frantic gestures came with it.

A dry crackle of understanding rattled from the old woman's lips. Bending low, she invited Hun into the camp.

Hun nodded, returning the gesture of good will. But he raised his hand in front of him before he moved.

Knowing every eye was on him, he walked quickly to the edge of their camp, bent down and sliced off a handful of dried grass with his knife. Next, he gathered up an armful of dried twigs and small branches and dropped them on the ground in the middle of the tribe.

Hun let the moment build before he went down on his knees. Not an eye blinked, not a head moved as Hun pulled out two blocks of flint and struck them against each other.

No sound was heard until the pop of a flame ignited the dried grass. As Hun blew it higher and added more twigs, a chorus of screams erupted. Hun pointed to the forest and soon a pile of dried wood and branches filled the middle of the camp.

As the fire heated, Hun took two thick branches with forked tops and dug their blunt ends into the hard earth. With them standing straight up, he turned and dragged the hyena to the fire. Three of the trees leapt forward to help him, then stepped back again when Hun raised his blade up high.

A quick slash up each of the hyena's legs, across its stomach and around its neck just behind its ears, and the pelt began to pull away from the meat.

Once Hun had it free, he tossed the skin to one of the females, then waved the old one over to the bloody carcass and handed her his knife.

The look on her face was unmistakable as her trembling hands took it and cut through the precious carcass and bloody meat.

This was his moment. There was no fight. No resistance. He would not have to take them. His spear and knife and the magic of his flint had already done that. And they had yet to taste the meat he had killed for them, roasting slowly over the fire he had made for them.

CHAPTER 38

The aroma seized the tribe as the meat sizzled over the flames. It was like a madness driving them to their feet and making their eyes roll back in their heads.

A crescendo of clicking filled the air and rose to a deafening roar as they shrieked and shoved at each other to be closest to the fire.

Hun took the moment and stood above the roasting hyena as the fat bubbled onto the firestones and the smoky tendrils of cooking meat drifted through the tribe.

With great theatrics, he reached out to the old female. She quickly put his knife back in his hand. Then slowly, making them tremble with anticipation, he sliced off an edge of sizzling meat and handed it to the old female.

She brought it to her nose first and seemed to swoon as it poured into her. Her toothlessness did not hold her back.

Hun's mouth turned up and he sliced off another piece. The old woman reached out her hand, but Hun shook his head no. Instead he walked to the leader he had first encountered and offered it to him.

The leader hesitated, but just for a second, then snatched the meat from Hun's hand and swallowed it whole. When he had finished licking every trace off his grimy fingers, he gestured at Hun and then at the rest of the tribe, making sure they all got a share.

Their full bellies made their eyelids heavy and they drifted off to sleep. Hun's head bobbed as he watched them. All it took to take them was a little meat.

The next morning, even before the sun rose, a circle of tribesmen stood anxiously around him. He jumped up, leaped back and, pushing his spear out in front of him, he crouched low. The leader bore down on his spear. He clicked at Hun and Hun clicked back, but they could not understand the other's meaning.

Hun stood up straight and let his defenses down, letting the tribesmen come up and take a spear and feel its point and test its weight. But Hun knew that holding one was one thing. Making one and mastering it was another.

For days he watched the new tribesmen skin their fingers trying to shape a stone. But chipping stone took more than stones. It took skill and balance. And none of them had that.

What had been taught to them had kept them fed, but kept them trapped. Their grandfathers had fed their grandmothers by looking like trees and standing still. It had kept them alive for all these years. Why should they do something different?

CHAPTER **39**

In the morning, before the sun lit the sky, before Ish or Lut or the babies stirred, Oohma got up, arched his back and stretched his paws forward. Fully awake and alert, he climbed the hill above their campsite.

When he reached the top, he turned full circle, sniffing in deep drafts of the air from every direction. The tribe no longer thought about Hun, the day ahead left little room for that, but Oohma would never forget. The anger he smelled all over Hun the moment he first encountered him stayed with him, as it would until one of them were dead.

But Hun was nowhere he could see or scent, not in the hills or in the valley, not on winds or on the ground. Not yesterday. Not today. But it was not yet tomorrow.

Ish was already outside his tent forcing his ancient back up straight when Oohma came back down the hill. When the grimace left his lips, Oohma rushed down at him, diving as he always did, between the old man's crooked legs. And like he always did, Ish rubbed Oohma up and down, playfully scratching him under his ears. Something that always made Oohma's tail whip back and forth in the air and Ish make his haha sound.

When their morning greeting ended, Ish turned for a spreading tree. He leaned against it and Oohma came up and leaned against him, sharing the warmth of his body with the chilly old man.

The look that Oohma saw had been on Ish's face for days. Making him sniff around Ish looking for the reason, but he could not sense its meaning. There were things he had begun to understand about them and things he never would.

For Oohma and the pack, for every other that walked the forest or flew in the sky or swam in the rivers, the future was the next moment, the next meat, the next danger. But the tribe was always looking over the next hill and around the next corner for what they didn't know, what they couldn't see and what was not yet, but might be.

A branch was something the pack would jump over or run around. Not a spear with a point of stone. A spark was a danger to run from, not something to be blown into a flame and warmed by. The skin of a beast was not just to be chewed through to get at the meat, but something to cover up with by day or by night.

Each night after the meat and the greens and grains were shared, the tribe sat and shared their clicks with each other. The more clicks he heard, the more Oohma began to understand that they were more than sound but had meaning all of the tribe shared.

One click meant *meat*. One meant *run*. Another warned *look*. And a loud angry one meant *help*. And there were other ones and other things Oohma began to learn the meaning of as Ish used them.

When Ish put his fingers in the sides of his mouth and blew out hard, a shrill sound like a bird flew out. When Ish did it, Oohma stopped what he was doing and came running from wherever he was right to Ish's side.

CHAPTER 40

Flint that could be worked was a treasure not easily found, but one that was easily ruined in hands that didn't know how to use it. It took all of Hun's strength to keep his hands off the throats of the clumsy tribesmen as the broken shards of precious flint piled up on the ground.

Hun's old tribe would already have scattered into the bush, reading the signs on his face. But the tree tribe did not yet know Hun and the snarl of his lips or his pent-up rage or the stinging power of his fists.

After days of frustration Hun knew there was no hope. There was no way this tribe, who had not yet even discovered weapons, could ever be relied on to make any.

As he walked away his fire cooled, and another way came to him. You didn't have to know how to make weapons to throw one. The children of his old tribe were not born knowing that.

Hun set off to be on his own, taking what was left of the good flint with him. It took some days, but soon he had made enough spears for all of the tribesmen. He put one in each of their hands and took them to a small clearing where he lined them up.

Before he let them, he showed them how. How to pull their arms back. How to point and aim. How to gauge the distance and the arc of the throw, the strength of the wind and how much strength they had to throw with to reach what they wanted. He threw some first to show them how and how far a spear could go.

Spears flew from dawn to dusk as the women gathered roots and heated them over the fire. They looked away when they heard Hun's screams and winced when they heard Hun's hands slap across their mate's faces.

Throw after throw. Miss after miss. Not one spear came anywhere near a target. If he wanted meat, he knew he'd have to be the one to get it.

He had come all this way and finally found others. There had to be a way to make it work. He'd look harder. Sitting there off to himself, he played it out again behind his eyes.

The hyena stalking them for the easy prey. Hiding in the tree to let it pass. His jump back down. The throw of his spear, the spray of blood, the death of the hyena, their stunned and shocked faces as he showed up.

It was all so simple. It could make up for what they couldn't do. And if he hadn't been in the tree to see it, he would never have thought of it.

Bait the prey in. Take it while its nose and mouth were tearing into the birds. The more he thought of it, the better he liked it.

The tribe would not have a chance to fail. All they had to do was what they'd always done. Streak mud on their bodies to look like the trees again, then capture some birds and put them on the mat.

But this time, instead of dragging them back to the camp, they'd leave the birds on the trail under a tree. Hun would do as he had done before. Hide behind the branches. Only this time, he'd be sure the bait was close enough for a hunter who knew how to throw a spear to come up with a kill.

Now he had a plan.

CHAPTER 41

Ish followed Oohma to the corral. The goats no longer scattered when Ish and Oohma moved among them. The she- goats no longer kicked or bolted when Ish reached down to take warm milk from them.

A short distance from the corral, Ish could see Lut's fields, their green blades swaying in the wind. The females of the tribe moved among them, some with thick, sharp sticks to pry out whatever Lut had not planted. Others used their blades to harvest the grains that had ripened enough to pick.

Today Lut would teach them what they pestered her to know. The secret Lut had discovered that turned the hard seeds they had gathered into the bread they all loved.

When they reached the center of the camp, near the large grinding stone, they dropped them in piles and went to work stripping off their seeds.

When they had enough, Lut came over, took a handful and spread them on top of the flat stone. She had learned how to crush them without soaking them first by changing the shape of her stone and twisting and grinding as she pounded. A few hard blows, some crushing twists and turns and a layer of powder coated the flat stone.

Carefully she brushed it into a pile. An excited click from every one of the women told her they understood.

Next Lut reached for a gourd of water and poured a thin stream into the powder. Not too much to drown the powder, just enough to mix it into a paste. The females crowded in, watching intently how much water she added and how hard she squeezed and kneaded the powder and water.

The paste became a ball and the ball a round in Lut's quick hands. While she tossed it back and forth, stretching it out as she did, the flat stone grew hot enough for the rounds to be pressed flat on it. The females jumped to their feet as the center of one puffed up and browned at its bottom.

Now that the females knew how, each morning the camp would wake up to the scent of bread baking and gourds full of warm milk Ish had learned to take from the goats. And now that they knew how, they would never forget and would teach it to their daughters who would teach it to theirs, along with the name of the one who taught it to them all. Lut.

CHAPTER 42

It took the night and the morning that followed for Hun to make the tree tribe understand his plan. Even though he explained it again and again, a lifetime of fighting and suffering for every mouthful they ate made leaving food behind for some predator to take hard to understand.

After many seasons he had come to know them. They were like the children of the old tribe. Everything he knew was new to them and needed to be taught and words would not do it. He'd have to act it out for them to make them understand.

The forest around them had many trees with branches that hung low enough for him to climb but were dense enough to hide him until he was ready to throw.

Every eye was on Hun as he dragged the woven mat close to the branch. Before he climbed up into the tree, he piled a few short logs on top of the mat.

Dropping to his hands and knees, he crawled forward, imitating a hungry stalking beast before he bolted back, spears in hand, and powered himself up into the tree.

The tribesmen's clicks quieted as Hun edged out on the limb. Any birds nesting in the tree scattered when he lifted his arm to throw his spear. The clicks rose louder as Hun's spear hit one of the logs and sent it and the tribesmen flying backwards.

Hun did not yet understand more than a few of their clicks, but he understood their confusion. So he showed them again from start to finish. He acted out being a tree and standing still and catching a bird and then putting it on a straw mat.

He walked around them, seeing if they understood. Then he climbed back in the tree and threw his spear. In the morning they would become trees again, as Hun had told them, and he would climb the tree and aim his spear at whatever came to take the bait.

The sun reached the center of the sky and a wide crack in the stone, sending a shaft of bright light into its den. It was a signal for the cave lion to open its eyes and pad carefully out sniffing the air for fresh death or something to kill.

The scents the winds carried made it roar and break into a run. Picking up speed, it closed in on its target, a pile of large birds with fresh blood on their bodies. Close by. Easy to take.

The tribe heard the brush rustling behind them and pulled in even further. When the lion came out to take the easy prey, so did Hun, easing his way to a clear spot between the branches in the tree.

It never looked up as Hun's spear flew down. But when the spear hit, burying itself in the lion's back leg, the roar was deafening. Dead birds could wait, but a living threat could not.

Its sharp sense could not be fooled. One look up told the lion where Hun was. If he could get close enough to reach it he could take it with one swipe of his paw.

A lion won't climb a tree, unless pain is driving its fury. And the two feet above him were just inches away.

Panic pushed Hun up higher, putting every inch he could between his legs and the lion until a loud crack from the tree trunk told him he was as high as he could get. He coiled his body as tightly as he could. But was it enough? Was he far enough away?

Hun was in reach. Just a few more inches and those jaws would have him. But that would take both back paws and all the cat's strength.

Hun was strangely silent. It was a hunter's death that was coming and crying out would do no good. What could the tribesmen hiding in the brush do but jump out and get eaten first?

The lion dug in its other paw to take a deadly swipe, but a roar of pain jumped out of it instead. Its wounded back paw could not support its weight and it fell to the ground with a crash.

It sprang up again and shook the pain from its body. Never looking back it leaped for the woven mat and the captured birds and limped off, its mouth and belly full, into the trees.

The moment he was sure it was safe, Hun jumped down and the tribesmen crawled out of their hiding spots. The look on their faces was undeniable. They had listened to Hun but all they had done was feed a predator what they could have eaten themselves.

CHAPTER 43

The tall walls of stone at the back of the camp faced west, soaking up the afternoon sun. Ish leaned against them, warming his stiff, achy body.

Above him on the sandy hill, Oohma was hard at work tugging on a root that stuck out of the dirt. It was a game Oohma had learned to play. Every time Oohma rushed at the root and attacked it, pulling it left and right as hard as he could, the haha sound tumbled out of Ish's mouth, like it did when Oohma spun in circles chasing his tail.

But there was something about the way Oohma's muscles strained when he pulled on it, something about the way Oohma planted his paws in the dirt to strengthen his pull that did not make Ish laugh. What he was watching meant something, if he could only figure out what.

Ish rubbed his forehead, let out a deep sigh and pushed off the warm rock. As soon as he did, Oohma stopped the tug of war and came running, leaning his hot, panting body against the old man before they set out together for the field.

When they reached the edge of it, Oohma followed Ish's eyes out to where the females were struggling with the digging tool Lut had wanted Hun to make.

Lut was right. There was no question that one long trench made more sense than many little holes. But the weight of the tool and the stubbornness of the ground were too much for them, just as the root had been for Oohma. Neither had the strength to pull it. Maybe, he thought, he and Lut could find a way.

When they weren't hunting or watching the females at work in the field, Ish and Oohma would go with Baba into the cave, sit down on a skin and watch him work. Sometimes when Ish watched, he took a stick and tried to scratch some drawings into the dirt himself. But no matter how hard he tried, all they looked like were scratches in the dirt. Nothing he could draw looked anything like what Baba put on the walls and the tents.

Baba's simple lines became living things, full of movement, power and strength. Whatever lived in Baba's hands did not live in his or anyone else's in the tribe.

His red-tipped stick flew back and forth as he dragged lines along the wall. When he liked them, he filled the outlines with grays and browns.

The more color he added, the clearer the auroch became. Ish could see its broad powerful body, its flaring nostrils and its long pointed horns as it grazed, staring defiantly from the wall. Even Oohma felt it and backed away growling.

As real as it looked to Ish, Baba wasn't happy. There was mood in his clicks and disappointment as he worked it over and over. He had captured the way the auroch looked, but not the spirit that lived inside it. Not like he had captured what went between Ish and Oohma in the drawing of them he had added to the wall. It held such power that Oohma went up and sniffed the drawing and gave it a quick wet lick.

Baba stepped back to where Ish and Oohma were sitting and did that thing Ish had often seen him do. Move backward and forward. Squat down and stand up. Lean left and right, running his eyes and torch along the wall.

Both Ish and Oohma watched the look change on Baba's face as something came to him. Stepping up to the wall again he laid down two quick black strokes along the auroch's side, hoping to create a sense of movement. One step back told him he hadn't.

Before he could paint over the lines, Ish leaped to his feet to stop him. Pulling Baba back, he stared at the two lines painted onto the auroch's side. They looked like the vines the tribe sometimes used to drag the trunk of a tree or a heavy boulder.

Uuums echoed out of Ish as he reached down to stroke Oohma's head. The females couldn't drag the digger for the same reason Oohma could not free the root. They did not have the strength. But what Baba was painting on the cave wall, near their drawing, did. All they'd have to do is capture and control one, like they had done with 20 of the goats.

The evening fires were already lit as Ish and Oohma came over the rim of their hill. The sweet smell of roasting meat and fresh baked bread drifted up to welcome them home and fill his heart with pride.

They had chopped a home out of the forest with their own hands and tools. Made each one a tent, decorated with signs and symbols. Each had a mate to sleep beside. Each shared life with one of the pack. Each went to sleep with a full belly. Each felt something as new to them as the pack of dogs. The feeling of being happy. And Ish's new idea, the one Baba had painted in his mind, if it worked the way he thought it could, would make them even happier.

CHAPTER 44

The trick was to find one. To watch its habits and how it moved, fed and grazed and most important, how it attacked and defended itself. It was one thing to hunt and kill one and another thing to take one alive and bring it home.

Once they had both eaten a measure of morning food, Ish and Oohma set out alone, as they often did. Sometimes late in the night, when the stars lit the sky, Ish wondered if Oohma understood what they were doing or what they were looking for. Oohma had no need to wonder. Whatever it was, Oohma knew where it was before Ish even knew anything was there.

They took a thin, ragged trail that ended above a wide grassy plain. The fire that had turned this part of the forest into a plain years before had left the soil rich and fertile and filled with wild grasses and stalks of wild grains.

The plain was not only alive with the plants that grew there, but with the animals that came there to feed. Herds of horses chased each other from one end to the other, stopping only to feed and drink. Lions stalked through the tall stalks of grain, their golden coats blending with them and keeping them hidden. Hyenas prowled nearby looking for any remains they could scavenge and steal away. But off in the corner of the field, what they came for stood hidden from the sun in the shade of a tree.

Even as far as they were from it, the auroch was a massive beast. Ish could see its confidence in the way it stood and threw its head around. It was fearless and Ish could see why.

The pointed horns on either side of its head almost touched the ground. A shudder ran through the old man. It was one thing to see one on the cave's wall, protected by Baba's magic hands, and another to see one in the wild protecting itself.

Ish touched Oohma in a way that told him to stay right where he was, at his side. They came to watch and learn the aurochs' habits so they would know how to move one or even if they could.

Ish asked himself questions his eyes had to answer. Did it stay off on its own? Did it graze next to the others? Did the herd huddle together, as the goats had done, or did they stand off on their own? Soon they would know.

Ish and Oohma crept in even closer, staying low and out of sight. The aurochs seemed unaware of them, too busy and happy growing fat on the grasses and wild grains.

Ish could see the one bull, the largest of them off on its own. Its brown-ish-black coat a sharp contrast to the intense gold of the grains in the field around it.

A distance away, three of its cows ate their fill, unaware that a lone bull, not of their herd and looking for company, was watching them all from a distance on the other end of the hill.

The lone bull watched its competition, the old bull, with greedy eyes and moved steadily at it. The old bull stopped chewing and threw its head up, its nostrils flaring with alarm as the lone bull's scent filled it. Its eyes narrowed, measuring the challenge coming at it.

The young bull was bigger, faster, stronger, more aggressive, in need to prove itself, but the old bull had been there before. Its body was covered with the scars of previous battles, its head and snout covered with gouges torn out by another bull's horns. But here it was, alive with its harem, while its attackers ended up dead on the ground.

The old bull saw the young one break into a run. It stood its ground, setting its hoofs and steeling its body for what it knew was coming, a head-on attack of a strong but inexperienced bull.

The old bull kept its head to the side, shielding the curves of its horns from the charging young one.

It was almost on him, just feet away. But the old one let it keep coming in, letting it get close enough to make a move. The move came suddenly, just a snap of the old bull's head and a sharp turn to the left.

The young bull froze for a moment as the old bull's horns pierced its body, driving its deadly horns into its 2,000 pounds of fury.

The air around them shattered with the young bull's bellows as the old one lifted it almost off the ground until finally the young bull pulled free.

The old bull let him go. Better to send a warning to any other young bulls that wanted to prove their worth than to leave it dead on the ground for the vultures to pick clean and keep secret.

SECTION

CROSSING INTO THE UNKNOWN

4

CHAPTER 45

The cows barely looked up or stopped their chewing as the two males fought. It was part of the season. But Ish could not tear his eyes away from the power and strategy of the old auroch.

Ish looked down at Oohma, made a sound and shook his head. He crept closer to where the smaller, calmer female cows were grazing and squatted down. Oohma sat down beside him and watched.

Unlike the old male, the cows ate slowly and did not push against or poke each other. They just kept some distance between them and ate the grasses beneath them down to the dirt.

But what would they do if Oohma circled one of them and tried to push it? Would they huddle in or run off on their own? Ish furrowed his brow as he watched them. They needed a smaller, younger female they could control, not a warrior with bloody horns bellowing his triumph to any bull within hearing range.

Ish's confidence grew the more he watched them. One, the smallest and the youngest, strayed the farthest and kept its distance. It was what Ish was hoping for. A single one off on its own with a space wide enough for Oohma to get next to and drive to their camp.

It was a risky move. But what had not been in his life? Their trek into the unknown? Letting Oohma get in close to him? Bringing the pack into their camp? Penning the goats in a corral? And all had worked out better than Ish could have hoped for. Why not this?

From what he could see, after watching them for hours, the cows cared only about eating, not each other. When one attacked another, no other auroch ran in to stop them. They just looked up, dropped their heads again and kept on chewing.

But there were things to be done before Ish and Oohma could do anything. A flock of goats held little threat, but one auroch could take down an entire tribe.

Ish rolled a short length of vine in his hand as he often did when he tried to think. Even if Oohma could get behind one and push it, making it do what he wanted was going to take some doing.

A hungry stinging insect looked at Ish with lust and buzzed around his head, looking for a place to land. The salt of Ish's sweat and blood was too tempting to let get away. It landed and Ish swatted at it, but it would only fly off a few feet, then come back in.

First it tried Ish's arm, landing just below his elbow. Ish swung at it, but all his hard slap did was leave behind an angry red mark on his arm.

Intent on Ish, the stinger buzzed in again, this time aiming for his neck. Ish felt it land and settle. He threw the vine he was holding over his head and around his neck and pulled it hard.

Flying up over the vine, the insect lifted its stinger, dove down and plunged it in, releasing its painful toxins into Ish's neck. Ish didn't notice or blink.

Even after another one delivered a second sting, he stood there with a distant look on his face. The cow's short horns would be the perfect place to throw a vine so he could pull at it while Oohma pushed at it from behind.

CHAPTER 46

The idea still worked, even though it hadn't. Why roam the forest for prey when the prey can come to you? That could make one man with a spear more effective than an entire tribe who couldn't make one or throw one with any hope of success. They just had to move the bait close enough to him so his throw would be shorter and better.

Hun had stopped trying to teach them how to chip a stone. Instead he taught them the magic of flint and fire. At least then, when he headed out to bring something down, a fire that could cook it would be ready when he returned.

The taste of bird made Hun yearn for home. With its smell of rich broths and stews Lut would stand above, stirring. With its game he did not have to take himself. With the crackle of prey sizzling over the fires and the sounds of the twins that should have been his and Lut's.

Finally Hun fell asleep, but his nightly demons kept tormenting him. They came at him in different ways, in different disguises but the story never changed.

Bent old Ish with young ripe Lut. It drove him from his sleeping skin even though it was the middle of the night.

Angry but groggy, Hun sucked in deep breaths to calm his pounding heart and leaned against a cool stone to stop his sweat. All was quiet except for the night birds and insects chirping out their mating songs.

At first he wasn't sure he had heard it. It might have been nothing but the wind in the trees. But then it came again, from high off in the hills, a lonely howl.

Hun fixed the spot he was sure the howl came from. He memorized the landscape, the shape of rocks, the crooked trunks of trees, how high up he thought the howl had come from so he could find the spot again once it was light.

He felt a wave of peace come over him as he ran it through again and again. If Oohma could make Ish a great hunter again, what could another Oohma do for a great hunter like himself?

He could outrun the old man, outthrow the old man, outwork the old man and show Lut what a real man could do. If the old man had tamed a wolf, why would he not do that better too?

CHAPTER 47

Oohma and Ish sat without moving, studying the habits of the female aurochs until they could no longer be seen in the growing darkness. They watched them graze, what they ate and what they didn't, but especially how they lay down and rested, staying far apart from the others.

The touch of Ish's hand on Oohma's head told as much as sight or sound. He could feel a lightness ooze out of Ish as they walked back. He could smell his excitement under his calm.

That did not surprise Oohma. He had come to expect the unexpected and what had never been came into being in front of his eyes. Still, would taking a beast that big and that strong and putting it to work, work? He could only trust Ish and see.

The females had left the heavy digging tool in the trench, but for all their effort they had only scratched the surface, moving it just a few feet through the hard earth. The skins they wore were soaked through with sweat, their hands covered with scabs and dirt. Their legs trembled with exhaustion and still there was work to be done. Woman's work.

Ish did not sleep that night even though twice Lut had fed him potions to help him. As soon as the first streaks of dawn lit the sky, he was up and outside, Oohma right there beside him.

Before they set out, Ish did as he usually did and looked over his shoulder to be sure they were alone. No one, even Lut, needed to know what he was thinking until he was ready to do it. If it worked no words would be needed and if it didn't no one needed to know.

When they reached a small clearing, Ish called for Oohma to come close so he could see what the night had shown him. He took some lengths of vine and began to unroll them. Oohma took two steps toward him and jumped back, every instinct in his body bristling with high alert when he saw them.

Since Oohma had taken his first steps out of his litter, he had roamed free, never tied, never corralled. And he was not going to allow himself to be captured and tied.

He looked over at Ish and let out a low warning growl. Was the old man he trusted so deeply not to be trusted any more?

Ish saw Oohma's reaction and quickly knelt down in front of him, making soothing sounds and rubbing his sides and head.

Oohma drew in deep drafts of air, reading the signals Ish's body released. There was no anger, no aggression, nothing, it seemed, to fear.

Slowly Ish put the vine around Oohma's neck and let him get used to its feel. Once Oohma calmed, Ish gave the vine a tug and Oohma moved forward. Another tug, another few steps. Then Ish took the ends of the vine and tied them around a log that had fallen at the edge of the trail.

Ish came around and tugged at the vine. Oohma strained every muscle in his body until the log began to move. The more it moved, the easier it became. When it did, he took the vine off Oohma's neck and buried his chin in Oohma's fur.

It would work. He knew it would. He just needed something bigger and stronger than Oohma to help the females pull the digging tool through the hard earth. And he knew just where one was calmly feeding.

CHAPTER 48

Hun felt worn to the bone. He needed to stop to rest and eat and think. The mountains had not seemed so far away when he started out, but no matter how far he walked, they didn't get any closer.

He found a shady spot near a giant pine where the fallen needles made a soft spot to lie down in. He put some of the driest ones off to the side and got out his flint. Once a fire had started, he took his spear and set out to find something to cook over it.

The only eggs in the tree nests he could find were empty, nothing but cracked shells. The mole tunnels he could see on the ground were as free of moles as the rabbit warrens were of rabbits. Hungrily, he stripped a few berries from the thorny bushes at the edge of the clearing. They gave him the strength he needed to walk up the next hill.

From atop, he could see a small stream and the outline of other hills against the still far-off mountains. A sense of relief spread over him. The howls he had heard in the night came from the hills he was close to, not from the mountains still so far away.

The flash of fish darting from the shadows of the stream bank after bugs and flies were just below the surface. Spear in hand, he waded into the icy knee-deep water and waited for one to settle.

His legs had numbed and his knees turned blue before he saw the first one jump. A bolt of energy filled his body and he jumped after the fish but landed short on a moss-covered rock he could not hold on to.

Yelping, he muscled himself up out of the stream, choking and soaking wet. But he shook it off. His anger could wait until his stomach was full.

The sun was setting and the night insects were waking up, leaving their nests and swooping low over the stream bed and that waiting trout below.

Hun saw one move to the middle of the stream without noticing that his legs were there. The flies were much more interesting.

The trout made its move and Hun made his. As the fish caught the air, Hun caught the fish on the end of his spear. He could feel the weight of it as it flapped to free itself and he leaped out to get it to the safety of the land.

Nothing ever felt as good as the flames of the fire warming his shivering skin. Nothing ever tasted as good as the trout did that night as he tore off crispy chunks and stuffed them into his mouth.

Bones and all he ate it, then drank until he could hold no more and sat back again to wait for the moon, almost full again, to move above the jagged mountains.

His head shook sadly as he watched it, knowing how many had already passed from sliver to full since he had left the old tribe behind. He was safe and he had slept and eaten with the new tribe, but he was not of them. Their ways were not his ways and their home was not his home. It would never be, no matter how many seasons had passed.

A howl, sad and lonely, cut through the cool air of the night just as Hun hoped it would and carried what Hun was hoping to hear. A single howl, from a single wolf, one that could be to him what Oohma was to Ish and Lut. Soon he'd find it. Soon it would be his, and then all he dreamed of would be his and more.

CHAPTER 49

Ish called for the hunters with a pounding of his hands on the drum and a loud shrieking yell. In seconds they surrounded him, spears in hand, questions on their faces. He clicked some anxious sounds at them and drew pictures in the air with his fingers, using sweeping motions to explain what his words could not.

The look on the tribesmen's faces was unmistakable. All their heads shook back and forth together. Capturing an auroch could not be done. It was too big, too strong, too fierce.

Still they would do what Ish told them to. Ish and Oohma had taken wild goats and put them in a pen and Lut had made the forest a field and seeds bread. And that could not be done until it was.

They followed Ish and Oohma down the trail, their faces frozen with fear. More than once, Ish turned back to silence their clicking questions. They all knew never to let their prey know they are coming for it, but they were too worried to stay still.

They reached the meadow when the sun was still high and hot and the old male was lying down in the shade of a tree. All but one of the cows, the smallest of them, was grazing at the middle of the meadows.

Ish crawled back and signaled to the tribesmen to crawl with him close to the meadow's edge. He pointed at the big male and waved his hands no, then at the females and waved no again. But then he pointed to the young one, off by itself and shook his head yes.

Now the tribesmen understood why Ish was carrying a long length of vine with him. But they hoped they were wrong.

The old male and the other cows barely reacted as Ish and Oohma stepped carefully into the field. Even a small female could handle the much smaller animal moving behind her and the bent old one coming up in front.

While the cow was looking back at Oohma, Ish sprang forward and threw the vine at it. To Ish's great surprise the cow didn't turn to him when it felt the vine, but kept looking backward. The threat behind it was greater.

In a heartbeat the docile young cow felt Oohma snapping at its hoofs and became a raging bull. It spun and charged at Oohma, horns down, trails of steam shooting out of its snout. Oohma reacted to her move with one of his own. He jumped back quickly to his left, sure the young auroch was coming at his right, but he was wrong.

The auroch jammed her horns underneath Oohma and reared up, tossing Oohma high into the air before it backed away and rumbled toward the other cows across the meadow.

Oohma came down hard with a thud, a sharp yowl, a long whimper, a stream of blood. Then nothing. No sounds. No movement. No sign of life.

CHAPTER 50

Screams of anguish flew from Ish as he hobbled to Oohma's limp body and dragged him from the meadow into the tall grass.

He spread Oohma's fur with frantic fingers and pressed his ear in tight to his chest until he heard it, faint and irregular. Oohma's heart still beat.

Ish waved one of the tribesmen over, a young reedy hunter, the fastest in the tribe, and made the lift-up gesture. The young hunter bent down and scooped Oohma up. Ish pushed at him and he ran back to the camp and Lut.

Lut was stripping leaves outside her healing tent when the runner rounded the hilltop, Oohma's limp body in his trembling arms.

Filled with terror, she threw back the flap of her tent and waved the runner in. Her face drew tight and her eyes grew wet as she scanned Oohma's broken body. He was alive, but just barely.

Lut ran her practiced eyes over him, pushed aside his coat and lifted his paws. He had some punctures but not too deep. Luck had been with him. The auroch's horns had gone under him, not into him.

As gently as she could she touched him, the length of his body, his legs and finally his skull. She could feel no sharp edges and detect no breaks or anything poking out of place. The force of the fall had knocked the wind from his lungs and knocked him out. He was hurt but breathing and whole.

Lut took some of the wild lettuce tea she kept in a hollow gourd and drew some into her mouth. Crawling to Oohma's side, she lifted his lip and blew the tea into his.

Two more times she blew in lettuce tea and she sat back to wait. Long moments passed, day turned to night until she heard a sound other than her heart. It was the breathing of Oohma getting stronger.

Lut squealed a happy sound and Ish burst inside. A pain seared through him when he saw Oohma still lying there, his coat bloody, his eyes still closed.

Lut turned around to face Ish and his heart dropped, not knowing what she would say. His hand was shaking like a branch as she reached out to touch him.

Taking Ish's hand, she put it on Oohma's chest, just above his heart. It choked his throat when he felt it still beat and Lut let him know she could save him.

Quickly Lut took more yellow yarrow and ground it into a paste and pressed it into Oohma's wounds. She could see the lettuce tea was taking effect. His body relaxed as the pain released its grip.

Lut rubbed Oohma's head gently and placed a skin soaked in one of her potions over his head and eyes. As he stilled, she whispered in his ear that she and Ish were there and he was safe and alive.

After some hours Oohma's lids fluttered and his paws drew in close to his body. His eyes opened just a slit, just wide enough to see Lut kneeling over him, sending her energy into him.

He pressed back against the pain and pressed his head against her hand with the little energy he had regained. He whimpered and fell back into a deep, sound sleep.

With Oohma asleep, Lut reached over and took Ish's hand and pressed it to her tear-streaked face. Ish was pale and laboring to breathe. Both had lost things close to them before but never had it felt like this. Never was there such sorrow.

Ish turned and crawled to the back of the tent. He did not want Lut to see the tears spilling from his eyes or hear the moans of pained relief popping from his mouth.

Turning, Lut left the tent. A deep breath of the clean, fresh air cleared her head and brought her knowledge. She had always thought a man proved his strength by feeling pain and not showing it, but now she knew she'd been wrong.

CHAPTER 51

Even though he had watched through gritted teeth and muttered curses, Hun knew Oohma's habits well. He knew how he hunted, how fast he could run. How high he could jump, how he rested and slept and what he ate.

The one in the hills could not be that different. Why wouldn't the meaty bones that Oohma loved so well work as well on the lone wolf and lure it in? Why else would Oohma have come to the old hunter in the first place, if not for food and bones?

But first he would have to track some prey and bring it down, alone, in an unknown place. He set out some snares he had made from strips of deer hide and scraped out holes that he covered with sticks and leaves, hoping something good would fall in.

A trail of spore gave him hope. It led Hun to a small stream blocked by piles of sticks that stretched from one bank to the other.

Hun slipped behind a wide boulder and sank to his knees. He had seen things like that before as he trekked through the forest. But he'd always thought it was the stream or the river itself that made it, using branches that fell into the water.

Now he knew differently. It wasn't the stream that had made what he was looking at, but something long and brown and wet.

He squinted to be sure of what he was seeing. That it was not a rock or a log but a long-haired animal with a stick between its large yellow teeth. He watched the animal swim up, then crawl up and drop its stick on the pile and go back for another. Hun had a knife and a spear. Now he needed a plan.

He backed away to a shady spot and leaned against an oak and closed his eyes. The answer came to him like he was seeing it in a dream.

A small pile of rocks was next to his leg. He picked up a handful and waited for the animal to come swimming back.

When it did, Hun threw a small rock into the water behind it and stood up tall to see what would happen. The splash of the rock matched the splash of the animal diving under it to safety.

When the water cleared and settled and no more sounds were heard, the animal popped its head up, took a breath of air and shook its head dry, ready to swim back for another small branch. That was good. It breathed air.

Hun waited until it began to move upstream and threw another rock, this time even closer, and once again the animal dove below the surface.

Hun slapped his hand on his leg, knowing it would work. He would throw a rock, watch the animal go under, sneak over the pile of sticks and wait for the animal to come up to take a breath. He'd make it its last.

Hun took a small flat stone and ran it along his spear point, sharpening its edges. He grunted and a rare "ha" jumped out of him as he rubbed his face. The stab of a spear was always truer than a throw.

CHAPTER 52

Oohma slept for three days without moving. All he drank was what Lut blew into his mouth and all he ate were small bits of her healing paste that she pressed between his teeth while she rubbed his throat to help him swallow.

When Lut rolled Oohma over to check the scars under him, she could see that the short hairs around his wounds were beginning to grow back and the scabs that had formed were beginning to turn dark and hard.

The whispers were right again, as they always were. They told her it would take time, but Oohma would live and be himself again. Now her fears turned to Ish.

He had not been thrown in the air like Oohma, but he was wounded just as deeply. He sat outside the healing tent, day and night, since Oohma had been carried in from the auroch's throw.

Even when a rainstorm blew through their camp, he pulled an oiled deerskin over his head and sat still. He could not share Oohma's hurt, but he would share the pain. If anyone other than Lut came near him, even to offer drink or food, he slapped at them, shoving them harshly away.

The feeling that had haunted him since Oohma was thrown into the air had crashed down on him like no other.

He had seen his brothers die trying to save their suffering father. He had watched mothers bury their babies and women die giving birth many times and all of that he accepted as part of life and moved on.

But this time Ish could not move on. He had pushed Oohma to push the female auroch from behind. In horror he had watched the beast turn for Oohma, ready for him, snorting steams of hot air, dropping her horns and throwing Oohma up high. Then the moment of not knowing if Oohma was dead or if he was still alive.

He had thought it would work but it was the mistake of his life. But his life would not be the one to pay for it, even though he wished it were.

Ish jumped up when Lut came out, desperate to know, but afraid to hear her news. The look on his face broke her heart, so she reached out and put her hands on him.

Ish looked at her with that look of his, and she put his mind to rest with a nod of *yes*. Ish's knees grew weak when he understood. He pitched forward and put his rugged face on Lut's shoulder, burying it deep into the fur skins she wore.

When his strength returned, he lifted his head, looked around to be sure no one had seen his weakness and went inside to be with Oohma.

Dropping down next to Oohma, he gently laid his hand on Oohma's neck. After he had stroked it a few times, Oohma stirred.

When Ish saw the yellow of Oohma's eyes in the dim light of the tent, a burst of joy exploded out of him. Hearing it, Lut hurried back inside.

Oohma was still shaky, wobbling back and forth on his paws, but he began to stand and take a few more steps with Lut's hand underneath him to help keep him steady.

It took some time and came with whimpers, but Oohma made his way outside the tent. Lut followed right behind him, bringing him a hollowed stone full of water. Oohma lapped up every drop and Lut filled it again, easing his fierce thirst.

After he had the water, Lut chewed some pieces of meat until they were soft and easy to swallow, just like she had done for the twins, and fed them to Oohma slowly from her outstretched hand.

Oohma stood a little taller after he ate and drank, and his paws began to steady even more. Lut clicked a happy sound when he took his first steady steps, and when she bent down to ruffle his fur he licked her face from top to bottom.

Ish knelt next to Lut, taking Oohma's ears in his fingers and rubbing them softly, something Oohma had learned to love. When he stood up again Oohma's tail swished, but slowly and he slowly circled the old man.

Ish blew out a slow whistle and wiped the sweat off his forehead with the back of his hand when he saw Oohma take his first steps. Looking up at the sky, he thanked the ancestors for not calling Oohma to them and made them a promise in return. He'd talk to Lut before he tried anything new and see what she thought first.

CHAPTER 53

Hun stood on the edge of the stream, blending into a tree. He had learned enough from the tribe's skills with mud to become part of the trunk. Too thick to be chewed through, he did not merit a second look from the animal in the stream.

Hun let it come and go, settling into a rhythm, lost to everything but the sticks it was piling on top of each other in a long, straight row. He had a handful of stones in his left hand and a spear in his right.

Hun's stone had perfect aim. The animal dove where Hun wanted it to, underneath the lip of the pile. The moment it went under, Hun made his move. Carefully crabbing across the pile, he positioned himself right where the animal went down.

He watched his own breathing, trying to gauge how long the air-breathing animal could stay under so he would be ready the moment it came up.

It lasted longer than Hun thought it could, but finally the water on the surface began to shudder and a brown, furry head emerged.

Hun was ready. He took a deep breath to steady himself, then plunged down. The air moved. The animal felt it and moved away just in time to dive under and swim downstream.

Hun waited, but the beaver did not return. Screams followed him out as he stumbled across the stick pile. They grew even louder when he snapped his spear on his knee.

Limping back to the spot he had been hiding in, he calmed himself, but it took great effort. Since he had met the new tribe, things that should have been easy never were.

His anger had a price and now he had to pay it. Though the forests were full of thin trees, finding the right one, one straight enough and light enough to strap a stone point to could take hours. Still he knew one thing. His aim was off, but not his strategy. Stabbing down was a much better way.

His hunger grew as his new spear took shape. Nuts and roots were not meat, but they would get him through the night. The next day would be different, that he promised himself. He'd have meat and he'd have bones, enough to fill his belly and enough to lure in the lonely wolf howling in the hills.

Hun woke at first light and hurried down the path to the place where he had hidden before. What he saw turned his mouth up. The animal with the long, brown fur had shown up again, doing what Hun had seen it do the day before, and the pile had grown even higher.

Nothing the animal in the water was doing was different and Hun followed its lead. Change nothing. Throw stones. Watch the animal dive. Sneak out. Wait. Balance. Stab.

After it dropped its stick and swam back downstream for another, Hun came out again. He shook the tension of anticipation from his arms and legs and drew in deep breaths to slow his heart, waiting for exactly the right moment.

He could do it. It was no different from others he had pierced with his spear and roasted over the fire. It could just hold its breath longer. Hun took aim and threw the stone.

It hit the stream exactly where Hun wanted it to and the moment the animal went under, Hun was running for the pile, arms spread wide to balance him. With no sound or shake to scare it, he made his way to the spot where the beaver usually surfaced and stood perfectly still.

CHAPTER 54

The twins were like nothing any of the tribe had ever seen before. There was no female who did not recognize that Lut's babies were far beyond any of the others in the tribe.

They walked before they should have. They babbled back the clicks the tribe made before any other baby could. As the months and years passed, they understood things before they were shown, or learned on the first try.

No one in the tribe found that strange. Both Lut and Ish were the makers of miracles, how could their children not be so? And there were two of them, identical in look, but each possessing skills and strengths of their own.

The tribe took its meaning as they gossiped with each other. Ish's powers and Lut's skills and knowledge were too much for one child. It had to be shared by two.

A warm feeling spread over Lut as she saw the respect even the elders showed her children. Pride was not a good thing in a hostile world. It could make you drop your guard. But she could not help herself. Each time she thought of it, a sound like the birds made chirped out of her mouth.

Ish watched Lut, as he often did while she was busy with something new. This time, a hard chip of bark from a tree near the stream with soft, leafy branches that hung to the ground.

Lut had chewed some once before to relieve the throb in her tooth, but she had thought it was chewing the bark, not what was in the bark that took the throb away. But now she knew differently as the pain in her shoulders from crushing for hours began to fade.

While Lut was busy with her grinding bowl, Ish took the twins by their hands and walked to the field. He was not sure they would understand what he would show them, but they needed to see what their mother had done. It was not too soon. They were not too young.

He walked them between the rows of grasses and made them stop, stoop down and touch a few. When they had, he swept his arm around the field, then turned to the forest again, then back to the field and said, "Lut."

Ish let a few moments pass and again he swept his arm around and made them run their hands along the grasses. Stopping to strip some seeds, he poured some of them into each of their open hands and again, just as loud, he said, "Lut."

The corral came next. He circled it holding both to him, then lifted each high enough to see the goats inside and said, "Lut."

He had taught them much, but they needed to know where they had come from and what their mother had accomplished before them. Nothing less would be expected of them when their time came.

Ish straightened as he stood there. His body had weakened, but his memory stayed strong. He remembered the pain of hunger, the sting of pouring rain, the endless treks through the burning sun, searching as always for the night's meal and not knowing if he'd have one. That was a life the twins would never know. Still, they needed to know about it.

Lut saw the look on Ish's face as they returned and the twins rushed into her open arms. She dropped her eyes from his as a blotch of scarlet climbed her neck and cheeks.

When she looked up again her eyes were full of mist. She turned the twins around and waved her arm for them to follow. She pointed first to the tent they slept in, then to the fire that warmed them and to the skins they were wearing and then to Oohma, panting happily next to them, and said, "Ish."

THE LAWS OF
THE EARTH

5

CHAPTER 55

The cold stream rushing under Hun made his legs shake. The only thing knocking harder than his knees were his teeth as he stood on top of the pile, trying not to rattle the sticks with his shivers.

It had been under a long time, longer than Hun could imagine it could. But every being that lived on land had to breathe, this one too.

Finally a trickle of bubbles came up, then the surface of the water trembled just below the spot where he was standing. Slowly, cautiously, first just some wet fur, then a round head showed. Hun lifted his spear up and steadied his legs.

Before it could take the breath it needed, Hun took away the reason it needed it. He stabbed it dead center with his spear, skewering the animal from its chest to its tail.

When he was sure it was dead, he dragged it out of the water and along the stick pile to the banks of the stream. With a grunt he heaved the heavy, soaking wet body. It landed in the dirt with a thud.

Now that he had dragged it out, Hun took the time to study it closer. Even wet, the fur of the animal was silky and long and luxurious, becoming even silkier as it dried in the sun.

Hun had known before he crept onto the pile again what he was going to do with the meat and the bones. Eat some and use the rest for bait. Now he knew what he would do with the skin.

After the dirt-caked, blood-soaked stiff one he wore, the soft brown fur of this prey would feel good around his waist.

He lifted the beaver by its thick, flat tail and slung it over his shoulder. At the end of the path, the night's embers would still be hot enough to make his hunger sleep.

His eyes were everywhere, darting back and forth across the grasses, between the trees and around the large rocks as he ran. The breeze was up, blowing against him and scattering the scent of fresh kill to anything with a nose.

Hun knew that was dangerous. He pushed his legs as hard as they would go toward the fire and their protective flames so he could eat and sleep.

The embers, still hot, set flame to the dried grass. Hun added some small branches and the fire grew. He took a sharp swipe at a short, green stick and it fell, cleanly cut, into his hand.

The wound was wide enough to pull his spear free and shove the green cooking stick in, driving it all the way through the beaver's body and out of its back.

His lips were twitching and drool ran down his chin from the corners of his mouth, but there was still one last thing he had to do before he lifted it onto the rocks and over the flame. With his blade, he hacked off its tail along with its fur. It was strong and gamey and fresh with blood.

Hun grunted softly and put the tail in his sack, giving it a final sniff. What lone wolf would not want to get its jaws around it and its teeth into it?

He didn't sleep, not even for a moment. The air was awake with the scent of cooked meat. It was only the fire that kept predators away and not at Hun's throat. He could hear them all around him. A shiver ran up his spine and he threw another log on the fire to make it roar higher.

Twice in the night, he had heard it and turned quickly toward it. Narrowing the place the howl came from even more. He knew it wouldn't be long until he knew just where it was coming from. He let the old man come into his thoughts again. He needed to, if only for the night.

He closed his eyes and there was Ish, feeding Oohma scraps but giving him something more. Something Hun's hatred did not let him easily see.

The way the old man ran his hands along Oohma's body. The way he let Oohma push up against him and press his body into him and lick his face while he stroked the fur on Oohma's neck making his haha sound.

It made his lips go tight to think it, much less admit it, but the old man once again had been right. It was not just meat that fed Oohma, but the touch of the old man and the tribe.

Hun nodded and made his plan. He would let the wolf in the hills get used to him being there first, not trying to hide, not there to hunt it, but just there alongside it, part of the landscape, posing no threat.

Then he would let it get used to the scent of the meat he put there for it and throw it scraps and befriend it. Then just the way the old man had done, he'd pat its head and bend down for his face to be licked.

Hun rubbed his belly, knowing the meat and bones and tail of the beaver would do it. They would lure the wolf out and bring it in. And if it were as smart as Oohma, which Hun was sure it was, it would know easy prey when it saw it and surely come and take it.

CHAPTER 56

The pains came in the night like they always did, but far worse this time than ever before. It took all of Ish's strength to stop from screaming and denying the truth they told. It could not be defeated. Not with a growl or a spear or a knife. It could not be run away from. Not with the strongest of legs.

Still, to see the old one suffer, to know each day Ish's scents weakened along with his legs made Oohma whimper and his head hang low.

Ish knew it was true. There was no other way except to listen to the laws of the earth that existed before there was an Ish and before there was an Oohma or a tribe or a tree or a mountain. But there was another truth Ish knew just as well. Still he was here and still he would be until he wasn't.

His strength was still the things he knew and their reach was farther than any spear he had ever thrown, and that made him stand up straighter.

Throwing back the flap of the tent, he came outside, Oohma close beside him, and listened to the sounds of sweetness in the air as the little ones chased the bigger ones at play. Their happy sounds matched his as they raced past him, their faces glowing like the sun from daily food and care.

Sometimes when he lay sleepless in the night, he would think of the children. Lutta, he could already see, would be her mother, but with a far better life. Raised on warmth that came from beyond the fire, from the arms of her mother and the eye of her father and the love from Oohma and the pack.

Lut had seen the fire in Lutta's young eyes the moment they first opened. She saw the knowing in her small, round face as she grew bigger and wiser. Kept there by Lut's love and patience, instead of by Nuun's sharp slaps.

And Isha. It wasn't because he was his son that the old man knew the boy was special. It was the way he brightened with surprise when the sharp, stone point of Isha's little spear found the middle of a tree and the way he could tell Ish things he should not yet know.

That night Ish felt his pain ease and sleep finally overtake him as Lut slept close to him, her body and the smooth of her skin warm against his. Oohma heard Ish breathe his sleeping sound along with Lut's and his tongue curled up as he curled up at their feet. And all slept without stirring all night.

CHAPTER 57

With his stomach full his lids grew heavy, but Hun could not sleep. The battle with the slick pile builder had taken more than Hun thought it would, and what he had done alone would usually take a tribe of hunters to do.

Stabs of agony shot through his arms from jabbing down at the animal and lifting its heavy, water-soaked body and dragging it down the trail. His hands screamed from pushing his blade into its body and butchering the meat off its bones. His knees were bruised and bloody from his fall into the streambed and the rocks hiding beneath its waters.

There was still a flat, leathery tail, slabs of meat, bloody and fresh and handfuls of bones. Hun knew it might not happen the first go or maybe even the fifth, but he had enough to tempt with and could get more if he had to.

The moon came out and the wolf followed it. Its natural way was to prowl in the morning and sleep in the afternoon, then rise with the night. A loner since birth, even in the litter it was born into, it had left its pack as soon as it was grown.

Hun's heart jumped as a sharp howl broke the stillness of the night. He jumped to his feet and cupped his hand at his ear, listening intently. The moon, full and bright, turned the night into day against a velvet sky.

The moment the moon climbed above the rim of the hill, Hun saw it move in front of it and stand perfectly still. Pulling back its head, it let out a sharp, lonely howl.

It was what he was hoping for. The wolf had come out to hunt again and what he had in his sack would be just what the wolf was hunting.

Crawling low, he moved in closer to see it clearer. It was one of what Oohma and his pack were, Hun was sure of that. But in the brightness of the moon, there were differences he could see. That did not worry him or stop and make him think. Everyone was different in their own ways. Why should wolves be any different?

Crawling through the brush, Hun's knee snapped a branch. The wolf's head snapped up when it happened. A flash of moonlight caught its eyes, making them glow as it turned toward Hun.

The hair on the wolf's neck stood rigid as it climbed down the hill. With caution, not fear, it closed the space between them. What it already knew about Hun from the scents he gave off told the wolf there was little to fear.

It knew Hun's secrets. Knew exactly where Hun was. It knew he was moving in closer and it would let Hun keep coming, to satisfy its curiosity. But there would be a line the wolf would not let Hun cross and he went to lay it down.

It was just 100 feet and some thick trees and rocks that separated them now. Hun could smell the scent of animal and feel a trembling in his hand. Only a fool would not be shaking with a fearsome beast so close.

The wolf could smell the scent of fear pouring off Hun's sweaty body. It relaxed at the power of the scent. If he didn't hurry and kill him, Hun might die of fear first.

It stopped for a moment and threw its head up for Hun to see, showing him the thickness of its neck and the power of its shoulders, without ever taking its eyes off him.

Every few feet, the wolf lifted its leg, leaving a warning behind. Every animal knew its meaning: *This is mine. Come no farther.*

CHAPTER 58

The wolf finished his territorial circle and put its leg back down, then turned and locked its eyes on Hun. It watched how his body moved, listening to the rasp of his breath, reading the winds for anything he might do.

The scars hidden by its fur had taught the wolf the scent of attack and aggression. But the hunter had none of that coming off of him, so the wolf stood still and watched and drew in the air around Hun.

Hun moved carefully, one step at a time, conscious of what the wolf had done. The sting of it still hung in the air. Some would take that as a warning, but Hun did not. He had stalked all his life, more than once reading an animal's moves, so he could move out of the way or move at it in time.

This wolf had spoken to him. It did not tear into him when it could have. It did not drive him away, but told him something instead.

Was that the first step to having it come to him and walk beside him, as Oohma did with Ish? He dug inside his sack, then walked up to the line and moved along it, waving his arms in the air to be sure the wolf would know that he had put an offering there. That he was the one bringing it flesh.

The moment Hun's hand left the sack, the wolf's nose began to twitch. The prey had prey. That was good and he was offering it, not protecting it. That was better. Once he understood why.

The wolf was in no hurry, but its curiosity was up. Just like Oohma's had been when he first came upon the tribe. And just like Oohma, it was cautious, ready for any move, any threat, anything Hun might do.

The pounding in Hun's ears grew louder as the wolf came up and bent down to scent a meaty bone and moved to another. His heart beat even faster as the wolf took one in its mouth and crunched it between its powerful jaws. It sent a shiver through Hun knowing what the wolf could do to him.

Hun stepped back. He had known it would take some time. He would feed it for a few days. And then slowly, with nothing in his hands but bones and meat, he'd move in closer until he was close enough to reach out and put his hand on it just like Lut and Ish did.

Once it laid down its marker, the wolf turned back into the darkness. No lonely howl echoed through the forest that night. The wolf's attention was on Hun and it did not leave him. Size and strength don't always matter, as any animal that stumbles upon a live snake knows.

For two more nights it happened. The moon rose and the wolf came out. The moment he saw it come into the light, Hun waved the scraps in the air, letting the winds carry the scent into the forest and up to the hills.

When he finished waving them, he threw them over the line, but not as far as he had thrown them before. Bone by bone and scrap by scrap, he would draw it in.

The wolf was in no hurry. The scents of Hun's body were more interesting than the bones. A little more excitement had built up in him, but still no aggression, still no rage, still no danger. Still Hun was too filled with fear to fear.

On the third night, when the wolf took the scrap, instead of falling back with it, it walked up to the line, knowing that Hun was there watching its every move.

Hun moved forward when he saw it, but not all the way. He wanted the wolf to see him full on. Not hunting, just standing. Not attacking. Not looking to harm it. Not trying to trap it. Just wanting to share his companionship and his food.

CHAPTER 59

Now that Ish was staying closer to the camp, Oohma stayed with him. When Lut or the twins did not need him, Oohma climbed a short hill and lay in the warm sun, watching the changes in the tribe that seemed to grow around him each day.

Before Oohma had found the tribe, he and the pack lived as all did. One day at a time. Hunt and eat, stalk and sleep, mate in the season and die in your time.

But Ish and Lut and the tribe lived a different way. They no longer trekked from place to place, but that did not mean they stood still.

Some tended the goats. Some planted, some picked, some hunted and stalked. When they were not hunting, men made tools, skinned prey and pegged the skins out to dry.

The females took it from there, chewing the skins to softness, reaping the grains of the field, picking the bounty of the earth and cooking it over the fires they made. Baba, the young artist, added lines to the cave wall and Ish hobbled among the tribesmen, passing to them what he knew.

All knew their life had changed for the better and all knew what had changed it. None, even their little ones, passed Oohma without patting his head or stroking his fur. And Oohma never let them pass without nuzzling them back.

This day was no different. The children's touches brought them each a long lick that made them giggle as Oohma tried to shake the hot sun off his back. With a growing thirst gnawing at his throat, Oohma stood up and headed for the stream and the cool water that rushed through it.

The last hard rain that blew through the camp days before had weakened the stream's bank, and the moment it felt Oohma's weight, it failed. The slab of mud sheared off, taking Oohma down with it.

He jumped up as soon as he hit the cold water, pulled away from the slab of mud and shook himself hard. But no matter how many times or how hard he shook his body, the gray clumps of the broken stream bank would not fly off.

Climbing out, he pressed against a tree to clean his coat, but that just smeared the mud, driving it deeper into his thick fur. When he saw that all he had tried had failed, he tucked his tail down and padded back to the camp, shaking himself every few feet as he went.

Lut made a loud, clicking noise when Oohma pushed her tent flap open with his snout and walked in. He was covered with mud and she didn't want him inside. It took a loud bark from her angry mouth and both of her hands on his back to push him out.

Once she had him outside, she called him over. Oohma's tail wagged knowing Lut's hands were full of magic and her voice was soothing again. She brought them together with a clap of surprise when she saw how much mud was stuck to him. He looked more like a bear.

Holding his neck to keep him steady, she raked her hand through his fur, peeling off chunk after chunk of gray, sticky mud that rolled into a ball in her fingers. The more she peeled off him, the bigger the ball became.

It was the size of a coconut by the time she had peeled out all she could and it was still sticky and wet. Taking it in her hands, she saw that the shape she pressed the mud into stayed just the way she pressed it, even after a few minutes passed.

A look flooded over her and her bushy eyebrows came together as the mud let her know it would do what she wanted. If she could make a ball out of it, why not a deep hollow?

CHAPTER 60

Lut clenched her fist tight and pushed it into the middle of the wet clay until it looked like a fat gourd with its top fallen in.

She spun around it then sat down to watch it. Other than the color of the clay getting lighter as it dried, the round shape she made stayed just the way she made it.

Oohma trotted over from his place in the sun to Lut and her clapping hands. Touching his fur she felt a change. The mud that had stuck so tightly to him had dried out and was hard beneath her fingers. Lut's face lit up when she felt it. What she thought might happen, happened.

She scurried to the spot where she put the clump and carried it into the warm sun. Would it do what the clumps on Oohma's coat had done? Soon she would know.

Lut lifted Oohma's snout and looked into his eyes and he knew what she wanted him to do. Slow enough for Lut to follow, Oohma led her down the path to the edge of the stream bank he had broken off.

She held on to his neck with one hand and slid down into the chilly waters with the other. The large lump of gray mud that had fallen off defied the stream's waters and was right where Oohma had left it. It had not washed away.

By the time they returned with it, all of the bits on Oohma's coat were dry. Lut took her fingers and nails and rubbed hard against him, crushing the clumps and knocking them off, letting them fall to the hard, rocky ground.

She made her uuuum sound when she saw some shatter when they hit, and Oohma tilted his head to the side trying to catch her meaning.

He could tell that the crumbled clumps around him had taught Lut something she needed to know. The mud could harden easily, but break easily too. Even though it was hard, it was not like a stone.

It took her time and most of her patience, but the wet clay became dry and solid. Even when she poured water on it, it did not turn soft again.

Oohma could sense the excitement in Lut's body as she took some grains from a sack and poured them into the hollow. He watched her wait to see what would happen, but nothing did.

The grains stayed right where she put them, in the thing she had shaped and molded out of the wet clay. A pot.

She walked around it and made her happy sound. Every time she looked back at the pot, it was still a pot. Still round and hollow, holding the grains she had poured into it.

Lut's heart pounded as the visions took hold of her. If she could shape a short, round one, she could make one tall and slender or wide at the bottom and narrow at the top or any shape she wanted or the tribe needed. And if she could do it, so could every female in the tribe.

CHAPTER 61

The sweat poured off his forehead, rolling over his heavy eyebrows and down his grizzly cheeks as he came up the trail toward the line the wolf had drawn. The sweat blurred his vision, but not his view. It was standing there, head high, sniffing the wind, just like Hun hoped it would.

The days before had been a waiting game, sneaking up, reaching out, tossing meat and bones, sending out welcoming signals, but this day the wait ended. The wolf was already waiting for him to get there and Hun could not wait to begin.

Before he reached the line, he stopped short, weighing once more his plan. The signs he had been looking for had been there for him to see.

He spoke the language of animals, knew the meaning of cocked ears and raised scruffs, of bared teeth and snarling growls and all the signs of aggression. But this one showed none of that, just deep-set eyes that stayed on him as he walked up to the line.

Hun breathed out, knowing he was right. It was another Oohma that he could see and smell. That was why it had done with him just what Oohma had done with him. Watch him but not come close.

Lut he knew had magic. But the old man? The old man had nothing but years. If he had magic, why had he not shown it to anyone until Oohma and the pack had come?

He tucked his arms into his body, knowing it was more than a line he was crossing. He was crossing into the unknown. All he could do now was picture Ish and Lut and how they acted when the pack was near.

A shiver puckered his skin and shook through his body, making his breath come hard. He had never taken to any of the pack and they had never taken to him, but it could be no other way. If he wanted to take the wolf, he'd have to take the step.

The wolf had seen enough of Hun and turned, walking slowly back to its den. It didn't stop to lift its leg or remake the line. It didn't snarl a warning before it turned and left. It didn't need to. There was still no threat.

Of all the moments Hun had lived among things that could threaten his life, no moment was like this one. Every sign told him he could, but the wolf had the last word.

The wind kicked up behind him as Hun took his first steps across the line. It did not go unnoticed. The wolf was on its feet when Hun crossed it, and once it was up it came running back.

It was working just as Hun hoped it would. Now that the wolf had taken his bones, it was coming for the feel of his hand.

Hun reached out to welcome the wolf in until he saw the look in its eyes. He took off as fast as he could.

The wolf moved faster than Hun ever could. All that could save him now was hanging low over the trail if he could get to it in time.

The wolf extended its nails, ready for Hun's back. It hesitated for a heartbeat, but Hun did not. He leaped for the branch and pulled himself up, just out of reach of the wolf circling below.

It took a few moments, but with Hun out of reach the wolf lost interest. He had put a line down and Hun had crossed it. That could not be left unchallenged and now the challenge had been met.

The wolf yawned and turned away. He stopped to take a bone Hun had thrown him and slinked into his den. Before it fell into a deep sleep, it raised its head and let out a lonely howl.

CHAPTER **62**

Lut stood at the edge of the camp and yelled. Lines of fear etched her tear-stained face and her voice was coarse and raw. It was the fifth time she had yelled and now she began to scream. Both the little girl and the boy knew exactly what it meant when Lut called out. Stop what you are doing. Come back. Now.

Lutta turned and started for home the moment she heard Lut's call, but Isha was not with her. He had been right there beside her, but then he went looking for a red stone, the kind Baba turned into paint and was always searching for.

Lut grabbed her and shook her in panic, but that only made the little girl cry harder. They were always to be together, Lut had said that over and over, but now they were apart.

Lut put Lutta inside the tent and warned her not to move, then went out to call the tribe together. She knew her son well and knew the places he liked to play. The little hole in the rocks only Isha and Lutta could fit into, the stepping stone bridge across the stream. The thick stand of trees he liked to climb. Everywhere. Even under the fallen logs at the back of the camp, but all she came out with were empty, dirty hands.

Only one place was left. She ran for it thinking of the red stone and how much Isha loved Baba and the animals he painted on the wall.

Whimpers wracked her body. She could not stop and control them as a medicine woman should. But this was her little boy and all she could think were the worst thoughts a mother could.

"Isha, Isha," Lut screamed again, as she raced for the cave, hoping against hope to find Isha watching Baba like he loved to.

Baba turned for the place he had left Isha sitting when he heard Lut screaming into the cave. He had put the small torch he had made for Isha burning at the little boy's feet. But now, as his frantic eyes searched the vast open spaces he could see around him, he could see that both the torch and the boy were gone.

There were secrets hiding in the darkness at the back of the cave and they had called to Isha when Baba went out for more charcoal. How big was it? How far back did it go? What would he find when he saw what was hiding behind the shadows of the rocks? Isha knew Baba would want to know all of it.

Isha picked up the torch and felt its warmth on his face. He held it out and started into the darkness with its flicker to light his way. When he came back, he'd tell Baba all about it and watch his face light up.

CHAPTER **63**

*The cave stretched deep into the limestone cliff
with ceilings too tall to see and passages that
stretched off in all directions, into broad caverns
and wide galleries.*

A forest of feathery drips hung down and fingers of glistening stone
reached up as Isha turned a corner. The flickering light made him giggle
when the shadows raced around him, getting bigger as they climbed up
the walls. And there were more of them, even bigger ones that moved
even faster, running into the depths of the cave.

Next time, he whispered to himself, he'd bring Lutta and they would play
their hiding game and see who found who. An impish look crossed his
face as he looked around. Maybe he'd find one now. One he could hide
behind or wiggle into and never be found.

Isha's torch found an opening in the wall chiseled out by an ancient
stream that had dried up long ago. It was twisty and he had to duck down

to get though its narrow openings. A perfect place to hide. They both loved to play the hiding game and Isha loved to win.

Two steps and the flames of his torch went out. A terrified sob burst out of him as the blackness devoured him. He could see nothing in the solid wall of darkness, not even his hands.

Isha spun and turned and took a step, then took it back as his tears poured from him. Which way was out, which way went deeper in? With no way to see, how would he know?

Panting and screaming, Lut reached the cave and Baba ran out to meet her. With sharp clicks, frantic movements and red stained hands, he told Lut just what had happened. But he could not look in her eyes and she could not look at him.

Turning quickly she found a torch, set it blazing and ran back and forth, her heart beating wildly into every hollow and behind every rock. Isha was not behind any of them.

Isha reached into the darkness, stopped his tears and found his courage. He took a step, then another, until his hand found the wall's gritty surface.

A sigh of relief came out of him as he felt something solid he could hold onto. He lifted his leg to take another step and follow the wall, but when he dropped his foot down, there was nothing underneath it but an opening in the ground connected to a narrow tube that reached deep below the surface.

Isha's chin hit the side of the tube as he fell. Then his head hit the back of it and he was unconscious before he hit the bottom.

Lut turned and ran back for the camp when she could not find him. She needed Ish and she needed the tribe. But more than anything, she needed Oohma.

When Lut reached Oohma, his barks gathered the pack and they followed Lut. Their whimpers and yelps echoed off the walls of the cave when they entered it, but Oohma circled and quieted them. Their cries did nothing to help. They needed to listen.

Lut took Oohma by the loose skin of his neck and pulled him over until they were nose to nose, sharing the same breath. She looked in his eyes and said it like a plea, "Isha. Isha. Isha."

Oohma's nose was down before she could finish, but the scent of Isha was everywhere. The boy had been to the caves so many times, to so many places inside it and each scent trail pulled Oohma somewhere else. Even with his powerful senses the boy would be hard to find.

CHAPTER 64

Oohma stood rock still and sucked at the air. At the edges of his senses, off in the deepest shadows at the back of the cave, he could smell the scent of Isha that was the farthest away and the freshest.

His ears went up and his nose stayed down as he ran for it. That's where Isha must have been last. That's where he would start. That's how he would find him.

Oohma looked back for Lut and Ish and circled. They did not hesitate and tore after Oohma into the dark, their torches flaming in front of them.

Even in Lut's fear and panic, the cave left her breathless. It was like stepping into a dream. No wall was straight. Even the ceiling ran down to the floor as though it were crying tears of stone.

Oohma did not notice any of that. He was on to something with much more interest. His tail straightened like he was in a hunt. His nails extended, clicking on the stone surface, as the scent of Isha trailed on, even farther back into the gloom.

He could move faster, but Ish and Lut and the tribe couldn't keep up and their torches were needed because no night was ever as dark.

Oohma stepped down into an old streambed and dropped his nose again. Every suck of air was harder, making the scent grow stronger. He loped faster as it got closer.

The old streambed led to an opening in the cave wall and Oohma moved through it, the tribesmen right behind him. Their torches threw just enough light to drive the darkness back a few feet in front of them.

Oohma took a few steps in, then stumbled and pulled back just in time as a hole opened in the ground in front of him.

He shook off and steadied, then lowered on all fours and began to whimper and yelp. He had him. He could smell him. Isha was down there in the dark, deep hole.

Ish and Lut crowded around it. As relieved as they were to know where he was, panic set back in when they saw how narrow the tube was. Too narrow for any of the tribe to get through, too deep for Oohma to get down to and climb back out of with Isha in his jaws.

Lut turned to Ish, but no words were needed. Her face said, *Do something Ish*, and her eyes said, *Now*. He turned quickly before she saw his eye say, *How?*

Ish raced outside, not knowing why or where. He took a few steps one way then turned and ran the other, sweeping his eye for something, anything to help. Struggling to hold back his fears, he leaned up against the cave's entrance to catch his breath.

The scent of ripening grapes on the woodsy vines climbing outside of the cave swirled around him. He raced back inside and grabbed one of the tribesmen and pulled him outside without telling him why. Together, they tugged on a long stretch of grape vine until they had it loose and it was lying on the ground.

Oohma would hate it, Ish knew it, but there was no other way. He'd wrap a tight circle of vines around Oohma's chest and thread a long, strong length of vine through it, so the tribesmen could hold it, lower Oohma down and pull both of them back up again.

CHAPTER 65

Once the wolf turned and disappeared into the forest, Hun drew in a deep breath, steadied himself and swung down from the tree limb. The thrill of still being alive pumped through him, but anger soon returned.

Nothing had turned out the way he thought it would. All that seemed to make so much sense turned out not to make any at all.

But worse, Hun knew it could be done and had been done and Ish had done it. A bent old man clinging to the last moments of his life had tamed a wolf, stolen his tribe and taken his life away.

Over and over he looked it over and he could find no mistakes. He had let the wolf see him. He had come up calmly to it, showing it his open hands. He had hunted meat, butchered and cooked it just the way Oohma and the pack always jumped and howled for.

He had stood tall when he threw it so the wolf would know he had thrown it and it was not a lucky find. He had done everything right. Where had he gone wrong?

As his anger left him, the differences he had seen came to him once again. He leaned back and scratched his itchy head, remembering the first moment he had seen the wolf in the moonlight.

He had seen them, but his wanting it to be hid the truth. It was bigger. It was heavier. Its eyes were deeper set and wider apart, harder and harsher than Oohma or the pack's. And that could mean only one thing. Only Oohma was Oohma, and not every wolf was.

Branches breaking followed Hun back to the rude little camp he had left alone days before, thinking the wolf would come and set him free and do for him what it did for the old man. But now he knew the truth. The wolf was free and he was the one who was trapped.

Like it or not, he would have to do it. If he had to live with them, he'd have to teach them to be a tribe he could live with. They might be the only other tribe in the forest and bad as they were, they were better than being alone.

The little ones of the old tribe were not born throwing spears or chipping stones at their mother's breast. They were taught by someone who knew how, no matter how many times it took to teach them.

Hun stepped off the trail and headed for a vein of flint in a huge, gray outcropping he had discovered days earlier. A thin, jagged stone lay on the ground and next to it, a larger round one he could use as a hammer. After some heavy blows, he had enough flint chipped free to fill his sack.

Its weight wore at him as he walked. By the time he reached the camp, his legs could barely hold him and his hands bled from holding the strap. Some of the tribesmen saw him struggle and ran to help. But he would not let any of them touch even one piece of the flint until he was leaning over them with his hands around theirs, showing them how.

Once they could make one and once they could throw one with power and accuracy, he would take their one talent, their ability to be invisible, and use that to get what he wanted and not even be seen.

A sharp sound rolled out of him when he saw it play out in his mind. A row of trees sneaking up slowly on the old camp, their spears disguised as branches, their feet like roots. Before they even knew what was happening, Lut would be his and the tribe would be his and the twins would be his, and when he had all that he would have Oohma too.

CHAPTER 66

Ish slashed the vine in two. A short one to wrap around Oohma's body and another, a long one, to lower Oohma down and heave them both back up again. Coiling the vines over his shoulder, he and the tribesmen shot back into the cave, down the twisting channels and along the streambed.

Oohma was circling the hole, pawing at it, whimpering. But he stopped when he saw Ish coming at him with the vine. He dropped his ears and dropped his head but stayed perfectly still. He did not like it, but his trust in Ish and the needs of the boy were stronger than his urge to run.

Ish crept forward, showing Oohma the short length he would wrap around his body first. He held it out and made soothing noises, then came up to him. Oohma's skin bristled when Ish wrapped it around him. A short bark jumped out of him when he felt Ish pull the vine tight.

Ish hissed a tribesman over and put the back end of the long vine in his hand. The front end of it he fed under the circle around Oohma, pulled it through and knotted it tight.

Oohma's eyes never left Ish as he did it. The sweat on the old man's forehead was not from the heat of the torches in the narrow stone tunnel or from his run in and out, but from pain and hope and fear.

Oohma took a step forward and pressed his head against Ish's leg. Ish bent and put his mouth next to Oohma's ear and whispered, "Isha." The choke in his voice, when he said it made Oohma press harder into the old man before he turned and went back to the hole.

A tribesman switched places with Ish. His arms strained when he lifted Oohma off the ground and began lowering him into the darkness. It was so low Oohma could barely hear it, but Isha let out a moan of pain. That was good. The boy had enough strength left to cry.

The hole was pitch black but Oohma did not need his eyes, he had his nose. Ish fell to his knees to listen. He could hear him getting closer, the sound of his paws pulling him toward the boy, but was the vine long enough to get him there and back? Next to the boy, that was his biggest worry.

Ish saw that the tribesman had just a foot or two more of the vine. It had to be now or it would be never.

The stone tube narrowed even more, making Oohma drop to all fours and pull himself forward on his belly. He smelled the thick fur tunic Isha wore and smelled the fresh blood on it. It was loose enough to grab and close to his nose.

He pressed down as hard as he could, making himself as small as he could, then inched forward, the rough spikes of the tube biting into his back. He took one more painful lunge and he had the boy's tunic in his mouth.

When he had it tight, one paw behind the other, Oohma dragged himself back. The tribesman could feel the vine slacken in his hand, and when Ish gave the signal they began to pull. All the torches surrounded the hole as Oohma's tail, then his body, then his mouth, with the boy's tunic in it, came into the dim light.

Oohma's hot breath and the feeling of movement made Isha's eyelids flutter open and he started to cry. Lut fell next to the vine and held her arms out, clicking loudly to him.

Once they were both out, she was out of the cave's darkness, running for the light with Isha in her arms. Oohma had rescued the boy and he was alive, but would that matter if all she could do to heal him would not be enough?

SECTION

WAIT AND WATCH
AND SEE

6

CHAPTER 67

It was late in the day and Hun held the piece of flint in his hand and showed them again as he had since the sun rose that morning.

No, he slapped into their faces as he acted it out with his hands again, showing them that it's not the power, but the angle of the strike. It's the eye that sheers off slivers for blades and axes, not just the stone. But once again, except for one young male, the sack of flint was a pile of rubble.

The young male was good. Hun could see that he could read the flint and knew how to rest a piece on his thigh so it would not move as he struck down. He understood the secret the flint held inside it. What made it sharp is what made it brittle and that could make it shatter just as easily.

Hun stood over him and shook his head up and down as shards that could slice through hides sheered off in the young toolmaker's hand. Hun watched him take a sharp one and feather its edge gently until it was a slender point with a taste for blood.

Grabbing the young male by the arm, Hun pointed down to a thin, straight branch, an axe-sized hunk, and made the sign to chop. Two strokes took it down and put a look of triumph on the young man's face. He had made one, the first one, but not the last one. Now that he knew how.

Hun called the tribe around him and took them to a tall pine tree just off the trail. He stabbed his knife blade deeply in and twisted it until the point was covered with sticky amber sap.

Crouching, he cut a slit in the pole, pushed the sap in first and then the stone point. When it was solid, Hun wrapped strips of hide around it and tied a knot. Now, if only the young tribesman could throw, there would be two of them. And then there would be more of them, and then he would have what he wanted.

A sudden sound cut off his thoughts. The tribe heard it too as the stag crossed the trail heading for the stream. A shhhh sound leaked from Hun's lips. It's a good day when game crosses the trail.

Hun knew it would be hard because they had never done it before. Stalking with weapons, surrounding the prey, closing in, spiking forward, moving separately, but acting as one.

They fell in behind Hun. A few feet, then stop and freeze and then a few feet more, make no sound, make no move and move again.

The stag had antlers so wide and long it could barely get its mouth low enough to get a drink. All it was thinking of was the water below its tongue, not what was coming up on it.

Hun waved them forward until they were just above the stag, just within range, a distance he could hit, but then he stepped aside. Pointing at the spear the young one made, he motioned for him to step up and throw. If he missed, Hun could get another off before the stag took off into the brush.

The sweat was dripping down his face and his hand was shaking. Still he took a step forward, as Hun had told him to, and planted his feet wide. Hun held his breath as the young man threw and the spear sailed through the air. Time slowed down as it picked up speed, gaining momentum, power and force.

Hun let his breath go when he heard it hit and heard the bellow of the stag as the force of the spear plunged into its body. The tribe, seeing the stag stumble, broke into whoops. One of them had just done what Hun could do and done it just as well.

Hun stepped aside, giving the honor to the young hunter, who took the blade he had made with his own hands and drove it past the stag's ribs straight to its heart. When he had it out, he held it high for all to see.

Voices rang out in triumph as his teeth sank into the warm, bloody heart. Hun raised his head up high and joined in the yell. There was hope now and something else. A rack of antlers with 12 long, sharp spikes that would pierce any prey or enemy if it had to, just as well as a stone.

CHAPTER **68**

The bleeding was not as bad as she first thought, but that was only what she could see. What she could not see might be much worse. But that she would not know until she was alone with the boy, moving her hand above him, feeling his energy.

It was his leg that worried her most. If he could not walk, he could not run and if he could not run, life got shorter. Lut took it in her hand and ran her fingers along it, starting from the top of his thigh down past his toes.

She pressed down and Isha screamed out, but she sighed with relief when she felt no splinters of bone, just swelling and a color that grew darker as she watched. Turning from red to dark purple, blue and black.

She bit off a few wild lettuce leaves, the ones she used for pain, and chewed them into a paste she could put in his mouth, so even when he slept he could swallow. When Isha's breathing deepened and the spasms of pain began to ebb, Lut opened her tent flap to let Ish and Oohma in.

Oohma came and stood by Isha's side, licking his face and pulling his powerful nose across the boy's body. When Oohma stopped at a spot, Lut leaned over and made her uuum sound and rubbed more of her healing pastes into the bruised skin.

There was no inch of him Oohma's nose did not sweep over. And except for a few looks that brought Lut over, the boy, he could tell, was not hurt beyond recovery.

Oohma watched Lut unspool a few strips of leather and take two branches she had stacked against her tent wall and hold them against Isha's leg. A smudge from her finger marked the right length and she quickly hacked them to size. With that done she added a layer of healing salve and tied the branches in place, one on either side of his leg.

Laying his leg gently back down, Lut ground some dried willow bark into a powder and mixed it with water. Just as she had done with Oohma, she took it in her mouth and blew it into his, knowing that it took swelling and the fever down and sped the healing.

There was no more she could do for the boy, so she turned to the little girl, calling her out of the corner with a click. Lutta hesitated at first, but then ran into her mother's arms. Lut held her tight against her chest until the shaking stopped and the sobs dried up on the little girl's lips.

When she let go of her again, Lut went outside to breathe in the open air, leaving Lutta on one side of Isha and Oohma on the other, watching over him and each other.

That night at the fire, the tribe was quiet. No whooping and dancing or beating on the drum. The boy had been saved and Oohma had saved him, but what they had seen would not digest as easily as the meat on the fire or the hearty stews the females put in their bowls.

What was this thing they called Oohma? It was still hard to know, even though they had been living alongside him. Why was this beast that should be killing them watching over them? Was there another on earth that would take a boy in its mouth while hanging from a vine and risk its own life to save him?

When the fire began to dim and the winds grew colder, they drifted off to their tents. They did not know what to think, but that did not keep them awake. Ish and Lut knew and that was enough.

What they had seen, what they had witnessed with their eyes and mouths wide open would be told and retold and sung about around fires for as long as there were voices to sing. And then all would know and all would understand what had happened that day and what it meant.

Lut touched the top of the old man's head with her fingers and went inside to stay by Isha. Ish stayed behind at the fire and put his arm around Oohma and hugged him tight.

Oohma turned and looked at the old man and dropped his snout on his shoulder, letting out a long breath. The fire dimmed as they sat there together, sharing each other's warmth.

CHAPTER **69**

No meat was ever as sweet as the stag's venison that night at the fire. They filled their bellies until all that could be heard were groans, then snores. Any of the tree tribe who had doubted Hun or had suspicions of his powers put them away with their hunks of meat.

The next morning as the tribe gathered around him, he waved for them to follow to the blood-soaked spot on the ground where he had shown them how to slice the stag and take its skin. But bloody dirt and castoff entrails were not the point. The 12 long spikes on the stag's antlers were.

Hun made a *watch* sign and the tribe closed ranks. The stone axe the young man had made the day before slashed through bone and antlers as easily as thin trees. And every few inches, with every eye on him, Hun would stop and take a point off the antlers and throw it to the ground.

Even the least of them understood what they were watching and what Hun was teaching. The velvety touch came with a point on its end. One every one of them could use to kill.

They watched Hun gouge out a deep hole in the top of a pole already stripped of its leaves and branches. Their jaws tightened with anticipation as he drilled down a little deeper, then took some pinesap and coated the bottom of the hole. He let it sit for a minute, then pushed the antler point into it and wrapped leather strips around it.

By the time the sun left the sky for the day, an arsenal of weapons lay around them. Hun could feel their excitement as they stood there, each holding one, learning their balance and their feel, knowing their days of eating crow were soon over.

That night at the fire, one of them leaped to his feet and began to point and shout. He jumped across the flames and came up to Hun, his head bowed. The others followed and then songs burst out of them as they circled around Hun. He did not know the words, but he knew the meaning. They were songs in praise of him.

Hun stood up and for the first time since he had found them, he liked what he saw, a small army of warriors with weapons in their hands waiting to be told what to do.

Hun knew what that was. It had not left his mind since he first saw them, but there had been too much to take his time and his thoughts.

Once the spears were made and stacked along the wall of rock, those strange shells with the rough outsides and the shiny insides and the bleached white bones filled his thoughts.

A body of water that held creatures as big as those bones the shells were piled next to had to be known. Hun knew it would take a hundred of the flashing trout in the nearby streams to make one of them.

He held up a shell and pointed at it and a tribesman with a spear in his hand pointed at the horizon and a small, overgrown trail leading to it.

Hun clicked a loud sound and the men lined up behind him to follow. Hun turned and grabbed one, the one who had pointed, and made a motion with his arm that said, *Lead the way*.

CHAPTER 70

Day after day the smell grew stronger and a raw dampness in the air, more than any he had felt before, surrounded them until the sun rose high enough to melt the blanket of mist.

The ground changed beneath their feet, gritty instead of clumpy. When he reached down to take some, it poured though his fingers onto the ground.

His hunter's instincts would not leave him, forcing his eyes to dart around him trying to understand a world he had never seen. Each step he took filled him with excitement. Each step he took filled him with fear as stepping into the unknown always did. As stepping into the unknown always should.

He could tell with every part of his being that what he was coming upon was something big. Bigger than anything he had ever known. And if there was so much that was different already, how much more was yet to come?

In the middle of the next day one came rolling out at them like distant thunder in a sky without a cloud. A stream of chatter broke out behind him as the tribesmen heard it too. They knew they were getting close, just a few more hours.

Hun looked up suddenly, brought back to his senses by the squawks of the large gray and white birds with their curved yellow beaks that seemed to fly without flapping their wings. All of them were flying toward the thunder that grew louder. Hun quickened his pace with each step.

Step by step the forest thinned behind them. Dunes of sand rose up to take its place. They began climbing one, but to keep from sliding backward they had to drop to all fours. Once they crested it, Hun's legs froze as he stood there, looking down at the place where the thunder lived.

The winds blowing from offshore bit into their bodies and frosted the crashing waves with foam. And the sound, the sound they made when they hit, shook through all their bodies.

The tribe looked over at Hun to see what he might think, what he might do or say. But all he did was raise his hand above his forehead and stare, his breath coming in stabs as a body of water beyond all sense stretched out beyond sight. Any stream, any river, even those raging and flooding after a storm would be but a drop in its vastness.

Hun stood watching without moving, without blinking, as one after another, they rolled in. The sun, now a red ball, began sinking into the shimmering waters and the sky turned the color of blood.

With clicks and whistles the tribesmen pointed out a giant leaping out of the waters. A shiver shook his body when he saw its size and the height of its jump. Now he understood the bleached white bones he had seen with the shells as the creature crashed back down into the water.

A camp for the night quickly came together and Hun struck some flint and started a fire. The warmth of the flames felt good against the cold, wet night and they slept without waking, till dawn.

When morning came, the tribe followed Hun down to a sandy beach, covered with shells of all shapes and sizes and clumps of green seaweed turning yellow in the sun.

Hun's eyes were not on any of them, but on the circles of white in the small sandy hollows, left behind by the waves.

He bent down on one knee to touch one. The hard crust that covered the circle broke easily. He took some of the shiny white crystals and poured them in his palm. Then brought some to his nose.

It had no smell but the taste of it on the tip of his tongue made his mouth tingle. Hun took a hunk of meat from his sack and sprinkled some of the white crystals on it.

His first taste told him this was something special. Something as special as the old man's dog and maybe even more. Something Lut would want to know.

He walked a few steps but stopped when small critters with hard, pearly shells and pitching claws crabbed back into their holes before he could jump out and catch one.

Everywhere he looked on the endless beach, it was covered with life. In the sky and in the water and even in the boulders sticking out of the waves. As he watched the far-off orange ball sink below the waters, he thought he knew why. When the sun leaves the sky, it comes to live in the sea.

CHAPTER 71

The more clay pots the females made, the bigger the pile of broken shards became. And the higher it grew, the deeper the worry lines on Lut's face grew.

Oohma knew Lut was not in danger, but he watched her shake her head and heard her clicking sounds grow sharper as she stood over the shards of broken clay.

She could work the clay. She could roll it out in sheets and pound it until the air bubbles disappeared. She could piece the sides together and pinch them to make them tight. But no matter what she did, nothing she tried to make them stronger worked.

A sharp hit. Putting one down on the ground too hard. Forcing too much inside. Any of them could turn a pot into pieces. And water, what Lut had hoped a pot would hold, slowly seeped through the walls and out the bottom. It could hold some, but only for so long.

There had to be an answer. There had to be a way. Lut knew the pots would not have come to her to end up lying broken and useless on the ground. She would do what she did when she needed to listen. Go to the place deep inside her and do what she had done with the trees. Be her sister, then sit and wait.

Late that night as the twins slept safely next to Ish, Lut stood up and Oohma followed her outside to a dying fire at the end of the camp where she could sit and think.

She took a pot with a fat body and a long slender neck and put it next to the fire. But the low flames did not give off enough light for her to see it clearly.

Just behind her a pile of dried wood lay ready to burn. She pulled off more than she should have and fed the still glowing embers.

The winds rose up suddenly as they hit the red-hot coals. In minutes the logs exploded in flames. Too much wind and too many logs came together before Lut's eyes and spread their fingers wide. If it kept on coming and hit the brush outside the camp, Lut knew what would happen next.

Her mouth dropped open as the winds carried the flames across the stone circle and onto the pile of dried firewood, where it roared up even higher. The heat rolling at her was blistering and soon the skins she was wearing began to turn dangerously hot against hers.

Oohma felt it on his coat and immediately knew Lut was in danger. In seconds he had the loose hides she was wearing in his jaws. He dragged her back from the fire pit as the flames aimed directly at her.

Lut swept her eyes around them in terror. Anything that was not green was flaming red. In spite of the fire, a cold stab of panic chilled Lut and hot tears of fear streamed down her face. She knew she could do nothing to stop it. If the winds changed direction even a little, the flames would head right for the camp and swallow it whole.

Looking around frantically she took off screaming to wake everyone before the flames took their tents and her tribe. They heard her yells and when they saw fire, it stopped them in their tracks. There was nothing they could do but stand and wait and hope.

But Ish did not stand and Ish did not wait. He ran for a long pole and waved his arms for the other tribesmen to do the same.

The heat of the fire pushed back at them but Ish pushed them forward. Die now or die later, what did it matter?

They did what Ish told them, grabbed poles and started pushing at the burning wood. All across the fire line, all of the tribe, even the females, threw themselves against the raging firewood pile, knocking the logs far apart. They all knew a pile of dry wood flames higher and wider than a single, burning log. If it hit the forest, all was lost.

When they knew that Ish was right and the separated wood burned low enough to beat out and control, Lut was the first to do it. She let out a long sigh of relief and the tribesmen, covered in filth and struggling to breathe in the smoke-filled air, whistled out one of their own.

With the fire coming under control, Ish tried to pull Lut away. But she pushed him off, refusing to leave the dying fire until she was sure it was completely dead.

Her heartbeat slowed and the sweat dried on her thick lips as she sat back down. Exhaustion overcame her and she slept until the shuffling of the females moving with the new morning brought her to her feet.

She remembered the clay pot and looked all around her, but she could not find it anywhere. All she saw was a tall pile of white ashes inside the fire pit until the morning breezes started to blow.

The ashes stirred inside the pit, finding Lut's eyes and coating her tongue, making her spit and cough and rub her face violently. When her eyes cleared and she could see again, she liked what she saw. The neck of the clay pot sticking up where the pile of ashes had been.

Lut didn't waste a second. She ran to it and bent to lift it out. That was a painful mistake. The ashes had cooled but the clay pot still held the burning heat of the fire. A shriek exploded from her throat as she pulled her seared palms back and let the pot fall from her hands.

She cringed, knowing what she would hear as soon as it hit the ground. But all she heard was a thud and then a dull hollow sound as the pot tipped over on its side and rolled back and forth.

Lut could barely wait. She let it cool before trying to lift it again. The first touch, when it was cool enough, told her something was different. The grit of the clay pot was now smooth and the dull surface had a low glow in the morning sun.

She held her breath and pinged it with her finger. Then she did it again, this time harder, but all it did was make a low, hollow sound.

Lut bowed her head and her shoulders shook. She knew she had been gifted again. The pot, like the trees, had shared its secret and now she knew it was not just the clay that made a pot, it was the fire too.

She looked over at the last of the embers as they died and her head and her heart were alive with its knowledge. The fire was like Oohma, not just one thing but many. It could light the darkness and warm their huts. It could kill and burn. But it could keep them alive and let them cook and make a lump of clay a pot.

Lut put one hand on Oohma's head as she held the cool pot against her chest. Her breath came out in whistles and her body itched with anticipation to see if the pot would do the one thing that was her greatest hope.

Once inside her tent, she took an old hollowed gourd hanging from a pole that had water inside it and poured a long stream of it into the new clay pot.

She shook the water inside it, making it slosh up and down. But even after hours nothing leaked out the bottom or seeped through the sides. All the water she had poured into it had stayed inside it, just as she hoped it would.

Never before had something so small captured so much of Hun's attention. He gestured wildly, grabbing at all of the tribesmen, showing them what to do. Take handfuls of the white crystals and pour them into the sacks they had brought with them.

Along the beach the tribesmen went to work, each at their own small circle of white. One by one, Hun's sacks filled up, but soon one of the tribesmen began to yell. When the tribe rushed up and surrounded him, he pointed down at what lay at the bottom of the white circle. A fish, its green skin puckered but its body still whole.

Hun shoved the tribesmen aside and dropped to his knees. The fish he could see was old enough to have rotted and stunk. But it didn't.

Hun lifted it out of the white crystals, a curious look on his rough face. He turned it over in his hand and pressed it to his nose. There was nothing he could smell, just the sea.

Grabbing a young tribesman standing closest to him, Hun ripped a chunk off the dried fish and stuffed it into his mouth.

The tribesman winced, knowing how a long-dead fish could taste. But instead of a spit or a wretch, he licked his lips and swallowed it in one bite.

A look of wonder crossed Hun's face as his arm shot out and grabbed the fish away. He brought it to his mouth and bit into it until all that remained in his hand was its tail and head. It was old. It was dry. But it was good enough to eat.

The tribe stood on the beach watching Hun jump up and spin in a circle, stretching his arms out. They waited a moment while his cries filled the air and without knowing why, they joined him.

Once his feet touched the ground, he picked up his spear and pointed to the edge of the forest.

The tribe didn't think, they just followed, just as they had since Hun jumped out of the tree and killed the hyena. And just like then, they would wait and watch and see.

They saw him trace the short hillock of a mole tunneling under the ground, then lift his spear and plunge it in the tunnel.

Hun looked around and found a short, sharp stick. His arms strained as he shoveled the hard ground around the stick. He yelled when he had gotten deep enough to see that the mole had reached the end of its tunnel on the end of his spear.

The clicks of the tribe grew louder as the thought of meat went through their minds, but Hun had other plans. He motioned for one of them to bring over one of his sacks. They leaned over him as he opened it and began pouring out the salt they had gathered. A look of confusion shot among them when Hun poured the salt they had dug out of the sand.

He smoothed out the pile, then lifted the mole to his nose and sniffed it and made all the others do the same. He raised his finger and made a sign to be a witness to what came next.

All hunters knew how quickly a fresh kill went bad. How fast the hot sun could turn prey to rot. All knew a big kill did no more for them than a small kill because of that.

But something had happened between the fish and the salt and if the fish had done it, it meant it could be done. Hun stripped the mole of its coat, leaving only its meat. He pressed it deep into the salt and covered it over.

Motioning for another, he poured more salt on top. When he stood up again the mole was covered all over, top and bottom, by a thick layer.

He stood over it and turned his face hard, making a stay away motion with his hands. The sun would rise and set three more times before he would go and touch it again. He motioned for them to follow him.

What the mole could mean could mean more than anything that had happened before. More than the dog and more than the old man's tricks, more even than Lut's magic and her plants.

He would not have to capture her. He would use it to lure Lut in. She would want him for what he now knew and what he now had. A way to make the meat last for many turns of the sun and maybe even the moon.

The power of that washed over him like a wave. The dog had made Ish a king. This would make Hun a god.

The raging flames and their narrow escape left the tribe almost too tired to move. Ish and Lut looked at each other and both shook their heads. They still had a day of meat left before it began to rot, so Ish and Lut pointed them back to their tents and made the signal to rest. No one said no as their tent flaps closed behind them.

Lut tried but could not listen or take her own advice to rest. Every roll of her body on her sleeping mat sent pictures floating in her head and like Baba the young artist, who had spent the day pacing outside her tent, they would not go away.

He had watched her through the flap of her tent as she bent down on one knee, slapping at it, then rolling it out and kneading the clay. He had seen her wet hands smooth and shape it, pull and stretch it, then move it into the sun to dry. And everything he watched her do, he knew he would do differently.

He could not hold his hands still and keep them at his sides as she traced her fingers across the wet clay. His fingers jumped out and traced shapes in the air and he winced when she did not see what he saw and did something else instead.

If the air were clay, Baba would have filled the ground with graceful pots and animals of all shapes getting ready for the fire, alongside the simple but useful pots made by Lut.

His hand covered his mouth when she made a square and not a rectangle. He made a low click when she didn't roll out four small legs and put them under the fat pot so it stood off the ground looking like a hog. Why did she not see that the pinches she made on the lid could be a bird, ready to take flight with just another pinch or two?

Lut didn't have to look up to know what he was doing. She waved her hand and stepped aside, motioning for Baba to take over. He was standing over her block of clay before she could let her breath out again.

Lut cocked her head along with Oohma as Baba reached down and picked up a clump. Each time he reached for more, his fingers danced. Push in, pull out, press down, roll and shape. Lut came around to watch him closer as Baba went to work and, one by one, they came alive in front of Lut's eyes.

She blew out a sharp whistle when Baba turned and held it out for her. Her hand shook when she reached out to take the clay bear from his hand. It was so full of life and movement, Lut was sure it could jump off her hand and roar.

She knew the clay was as much his as hers, and she made a sign that meant cut in half. Baba didn't hesitate. He took his knife and sliced into it and dashed outside with his share before she could change her mind.

He was more like the twins than the hunters of the tribe, full of wonder and questions and dreams behind his eyes. When her laugh ended, a smile stayed behind as she looked at the camp and all the wonders that began as dreams. The circle of branches that held the goats inside them, the pack of dogs that brought them in, the fields that grew seeds that turned into bread, the purple flowers that turned the old man into a young man and the twins he planted inside her, growing straight and tall and strong.

CHAPTER 74

Baba liked the feel of Oohma's breath, warm and comforting on his leg, and the sound of him panting as he padded behind him. The way to the cave was well known to all in the tribe and especially to Baba.

That did not mean it held no danger. But with Oohma at his side, he held no worry, just pictures he could not wait to add to the wall and shapes he wanted to mold out of the clay.

Baba had brought along some scraps of meat, but Oohma did not need to be tempted. Whenever Lut or Ish or the twins did not need him, he went to see what Baba would bring to life that day.

The cave was like the womb of the earth and Baba knew he had been called to fill its walls with life. But before he painted more animals and shaped others out of clay, another thing had come to him that he wanted to hold in his hands.

She was the mother of us all. Stout and round with twists of curly hair on top of her head and hips made wide to ease birth. Huge breasts that held milk for all hung to her waist for all to reach. Thick, heavy thighs gave her the strength she needed to carry the weight of life inside her.

He would do what Lut had done with her tall clay pot and put life's mother in the heat of a living fire so the flames could give her the strength she needed to bless the tribe with life.

When it cooled he would take the great mother and put her in a small hollow he had dug out of the cave's wall in the middle of all the lives he had called from the clouds and put there.

Baba stopped for a few moments and lit some torches before he went in and went to work. He threw his head back and clicked out a song he had taught himself to sing. It was heavy with thanks and tears.

His voice rose up and down as he thanked the walls for letting him paint on their bumps and dips. For sharing their shadows and for lighting his mind with movement and flow.

He bent and thanked the paints and then the clay that Lut had given him, and then his hands and arms for what they had to say.

When his song faded into the darkness, he turned and touched Oohma's head and bent down until their noses touched.

Closing his eyes he rested his head against Oohma's warm head and thanked him again and again for the thing he had given him. The thing none ever had to give. Not his mother or his father, not his mate or any of his tribe.

The time that came when not forced to roam each day. Not forced to pick up all and move again. The time that came when the tribe had the thing it never had before. A place called home.

CHAPTER 75

For days Hun was like a mother bird guarding its nest, not letting the pile of white crystals be touched. Keeping everyone away but himself.

If he were right, if he had found a way to make meat last long enough to keep the tribe fed on a long march, all that he wanted would be his.

How long had it been, how long had he wandered, not knowing where, with no one to fight off the loneliness and help him survive? It was more than suns and more than moons, and leaves had turned color and fallen and turned green again. But how many had passed, that he did not know.

Still, when he closed his eyes, he could see every rock and every tree, every hill and every valley he had passed through, knowing that the day would come when he'd take back his steps and take back what the old man's dog had stolen from him.

That would be a day of songs and a day of dance and a day of feasting. He would show them flesh that still did not rot and stink after days and weeks.

That would be the day when he showed the tribe they no longer had to live from day to day but could hunt enough for a month and then use their time and strength in other ways.

A faraway look crossed Hun's face when he sat there seeing her face. The roll of her eyes when the first taste of salt hit her tongue. The sounds of her squeals when she saw that salt could not just make everything taste so good, but keep it good to eat. And that would be a medicine any medicine woman would want.

What could she think about the man who had brought that to her but good? What could she say to such a man but yes? Then she would know and then she would see that an old man with a dog was still an old man and he was not. What he had in his hand was even greater than anything the old one ever had in his. Even the dogs.

A stab of fear opened his eyes as the sun began to drop. There was just another day to go now, just a few more hours until he would know.

When the sun was high up in the middle of the sky, he would break open the salt and either laugh or cry. Hun looked around and headed for the beach. The minutes dragged by too slowly. He needed to fill his mind with something besides fear.

The huge boulders reaching out to the waves had caught his eyes when he first saw them. Now at the water's edge, he looked at them closer. Black shells were peppered all over the boulders from the bottom water line up to the top.

They didn't move or shake loose even when the waves hammered into them. That was good, Hun thought. It meant they were alive, not like the empty shells that littered the beach, and that could make them something good to eat. Just the thought of it made his mouth water.

He sat down on the soft sand and took the rough sandals off his feet and left them behind so the water could not reach them. Standing up, he peeled off his bearskin tunic, leaving only his loincloth on.

He had waded through the shallows that licked the shore. But the full force of the waves that he had only watched and heard, not felt, he would need to be careful with a force like that.

The water was cold and saltier than he thought when he wadded in chest deep and took an unexpected mouthful. He turned his back quickly to spit it out and clear his lungs with a few deep hacking coughs.

He didn't see the next one coming until it crashed on top of him, knocking him under and grinding him into the rough sand and broken shells on the bottom.

By the time he could prop himself up again, another one was on him, with another one building behind that. Hun quickly realized what he had to do to stay on his feet.

He tried to dip beneath the next one and come up on the other side of it, closer to the boulders, in the calmer water behind the breakers. He had taken the hit of a cave bear before, but this was even harder.

He watched another one gathering force, took a deep breath and got ready to break through it. He let go of his breath as he plunged into it, but the wave would not let go of him. It pulled back and pulled him out with it, putting his feet in too many feet of water to find the bottom and get his head above it.

When he finally broke the surface, he gasped in swallows of air. Panic rocked him as he saw the boulders he had been close to moving farther away. And every roll of the water was pulling him out farther.

He kicked his feet until he could not kick anymore and slapped his arms and hands on the top of the water until they could not move.

This was his moment. He knew it. He took a deep breath, his last one, and let his arms and legs go limp. Every hunter knew that he would die. But never did Hun think it would be a surrender in water, instead of on a pair of tusks or horns or in some animal's powerful jaws.

He opened his eyes again for the last time, just a slit. When he saw it, a dark shape, just beyond him, moving at him through the water, they opened wide again.

The memory of the giant white bones and the jumping giant flashed before his eyes. He braced himself as a thick spike on the dark shape's back broke the surface of the water.

Each roll of the waves brought it closer to him until Hun felt it slam into him, driving him back with unimaginable force. He threw his arms out wide, then brought them together.

With all of the strength left in his sapped body, he held onto the root of the floating tree trunk hitting up against him in the waves before it drifted out of reach again.

CHAPTER 76

The offshore winds turned suddenly, reversing from west to east. It was Hun's lucky day. The wind's shift made the waves calm and the tree trunk drifting out with him on it began to ride the waves back in.

Their clicks and yelps grew louder as they watched it coming into shore. It was almost close enough to grab. One more wave, maybe two and they could beach it, like the other pieces of driftwood scattered up and down the shore.

A last wave dropped the tree trunk on the solid ground with a thud. Hun's eyes opened slowly as if he were in a dream. He could feel the sand underneath him, no longer the rolling waves. But was he still on earth or in the place beyond the clouds?

He shook his head and coughed some coughs as his thinking returned, and with it his anger. Now that he knew he was not dead, he had to stifle the urge to kill them all. With his bare hands.

Not one of them had done more than yelp and scream and jump and point as the waves were taking him. Not one of them had come into the water to try and pull him out. That was something Hun would not forget.

Still, he remembered, he needed them for now. Or he would have left them the way he wanted to, lying face down in the sand.

The last of the afternoon sun finally warmed his cold body. And made his loincloth stiffen, then turn white, as the saltwater dried. His first mouthful should have told him the salt lived in the ocean waters not in the sand, but he was too busy trying to stay afloat.

Night fell and the moon climbed taking the tide out with it, showing Hun a sandy path leading to the boulders. The shallow pools the tide left behind would be easy to wade through, nothing like the pounding surf.

In the light of the moon, the black shells shimmered and the boulders were slick and covered with green fingers of growth. Between them Hun could see clusters of shells attached to the face of the rocks.

He reached out to take one but quickly realized it was no flower. It was going to take his blade to cut them free and then a stab between the tight shell halves to pry one open and see what was hiding inside.

A stream of water squirted into the air when he slipped his blade into it. A sweet, briny scent climbed up his nose that made his stomach growl. He cut the meat loose and let it spill into his mouth. It was salty one chew and sweet the next, with the smell of the sea.

He took another and pried it open, but this time he took a few of the white salt crystals and sprinkled them on top. His mouth turned up when it touched his tongue. The salt had magic and Lut liked magic. There was no doubt of that.

Taking a deep breath, he stared out at the horizon. He grumbled as he did it, but he had to admit it. He shared what the old man must have felt when he found Oohma and the pack and brought them in. The power to be remembered. Forever.

Soon he would know if he had it. In the bright light of the sun, he would see if the salt had done to the meat what it had done to the fish. Would it be rotted or would it still be good to eat? Would he be given the power or would he still be cursed?

He sat down near the fire and tried to stay warm and sleep, but the shivers would not stop and his hands would not stop sweating even though the winds were cold.

CHAPTER 77

Lut laughed at herself and shook her head at her own blindness. What good was a medicine woman who could not see what was under her nose? The swaying walks and swollen bellies of two of the females of the pack, their nipples beginning to stretch, discolor and sag.

She haha'ed even harder when she thought of the times Oohma was not with her and not with Ish or the twins. Now she knew what he was up to. Obeying the calls of nature to become a father like Ish had done and expand his pack. All she hoped for was that the puppies would be like their father, with as big a heart and as big a spirit.

Lut walked up to the pregnant females. Their tails wagged and they licked her face as she gently rubbed their bellies and cooed softly into their ears.

She sent her sister mothers a prayer of courage with her eyes and along with that a promise. Oohma had helped her have her pups. *She'd help their pups come into the world and survive their birth.*

That night at the fire, with her mood still high and light, Lut called the swollen dogs over to her. She lifted their front paws so all the tribe could see that new life was coming. They clicked and yelps rose out of them and swirled around the fire.

New life in the tribe. New life in the fields. New life on the trees. New life in the bellies of the female dogs. New life was everywhere, all around them. It filled her eyes with tears of happiness. And she was not alone.

Ish looked over at Oohma and his mouth turned up. Even this, the old one thought, he and Oohma would share together. He lifted his voice and lifted his spear and pounded it on the ground. The others joined him until the spears were like thunder rattling the earth and their voices echoed off into the air around them.

Ish's gruff face and his good eye gleamed with pride and promise. His little ones would have Oohma's little ones to grow up with, to be protected by and to share their life with. How much better would his life have been if Oohma had always been with him? How much better would the twin's lives be with Oohma's pups, grown and always at their side?

Lut caught his look as she sat there, her arms wrapped around the pregnant dogs. All shared the wonders of motherhood, their joys and their sorrows and the moment of excitement when a new life entered the world. Lut kept herself quiet with dignity, as a medicine woman should, but inside her she was dancing and screaming.

She could see the twin's faces when the puppies were born. She could see them sitting on the ground, squealing and giggling covered with the warm, little bodies of Oohma's pups.

Just as Oohma had always been Ish's, even when he shared himself with Lut, Oohma's pups would be Lutta's and Isha's. They would run together. Grow together. Hunt and sleep and eat together. And the dogs would watch over them, even if it meant their life.

A warm feeling spread over her that wasn't from the fire. She stood up and walked back to her tent with that look of determination on her face.

She was the medicine woman, whether to the tribe or to the pack, and she would do what she had done before when she had questions. Ask the plants to tell her how to ease the mother's pain and protect the puppies as she pushed them out. Lut could tell with the first touch of their bellies there was going to be more than one.

In the quiet of the tent, she calmed her breathing, waiting for the whispers to come. It took a while, but then she heard one tell her in a soft voice to walk outside and climb up the hill. In the thorny bushes, with the red berries growing on them, it told her she would find her answer.

Even though she had heard them before, it still made her jump when a plant called out to her. She turned, almost in a trance, to face a raspberry bush growing along the trail. She heard it say "yes" and knelt down before it to listen to its wisdom with a voice as sweet as its taste.

"Take my leaves and soak them in water," it said. "Then brew them into a tea. It will make the puppies come easier and quicker and ease the mother's pain."

CHAPTER 78

Hun was up before the sun. When the heat of it was directly over his head, he'd know enough time had passed.

He sat and chipped at his stones, but his look was somewhere else. Never had he wanted time to pass faster. Never had it moved so slow.

Anxious as he was, the thought of finding nothing when he got there weighed on him. It left him unsteady and his mind on other things besides the flint in his hand that he was turning to dust.

He looked around quickly, happy that no one had seen him do what he would have punished any of them for doing. Smashing the flint into useless shards like his two best slabs at his feet.

Finally the sun was over him and the sweat, beading on his forehead, dripped down his brow. He walked slowly up to it and sat down next to the mound of salt and raised his shaking hand above his head.

Instead of a strike, he decided on a sniff first. He bent his head right above it, making some loose salt crystals fly up into his nose. He grabbed at it, squeezing it tight and howling as he fell backwards sneezing as the raw salt ate into his delicate nostrils.

When the burning finally stopped, he brought his arm down with a sharp snap that cracked the salt blanket open.

His fingers flew in to brush the broken crystals of salt off the meat that now felt hard and dry. He lifted it out and rolled it around in his hand as the thrill of the moment spread over him.

Some things had changed. The flesh of the mole had turned a little darker and the outer skin was harder and its body was stiff and rigid. But there were no maggots eating at it and its smell was salt and dirt, not rot and mold.

Hun's blade was out in a second and he sliced off a strip of meat. The outer skin resisted his first slash, but underneath it, the flesh looked whole and firm. Another breath, slow and careful. No smell of rot meant it was good to eat. But only a taste would tell him.

The moment it hit his tongue, he knew everything had changed. It turned his knees to jelly. As he swallowed his first bite, he began to wobble and stumble.

The tribe raced to his side, thinking the meat was killing him and he was about to die. But when he saw the looks of concern on their faces, an explosion of hahas burst out of him.

None of them knew if he was roaring in pain or, as they had seen him do before, making happy sounds.

ANOTHER HEARTBEAT

CHAPTER 79

First a painful yelp and then a soft whimper made her walk unsteadily and made Lut jump to her side. She was weak and having contractions and her legs were spreading wider apart as she paced in ever widening circles.

Panting hard she let her tongue hang loose. The pain of birth was overtaking her and there was no choice but to let it.

After a few slow circles she stopped short and a spurt of water shot out of her, soaking the ground behind her. It was the signal all knew well. Birth was beginning and it was telling her to stop her pacing and walk slowly to a dark corner to lie down and wait.

Lut watched the mother scratch at the dirt, make a small hollow, sink in and steady herself. She watched the mother's chest swell with each deep intake of breath and blow out as the contractions made her bear down and push.

A whimper of pain followed each one of them out until the pile of wet fur at her stomach was eight. The mother knew just what to do. She turned calmly to them, bent her head and gently licked her puppies clean and nudged them to her waiting nipples.

Lut's feet barely touched the ground as she watched the new life come into the world. Her whistles grew as the puppies kept coming. No mother in the tribe could have that many and survive. She looked down and patted her chest. The puppy's mother had eight nipples, the female of the tribe only two.

Another squish of water spun Lut around. The first mother had barely finished and now the second was coming due. Lut watched her do just what the first had done. Circle, pant, then hide in the shadows to wait.

Lut's respect for the pack's females grew even greater. And they did alone what the tribe's women always needed help with. How did they know just what to do?

In less than an hour seven more puppies were born. Only six survived. The smallest, the runt of the litter, smothered as the others swarmed to their mother's breast.

Still, Lut threw her hands to her face and spun in circles, yelping her happy song. Fourteen new lives that would live alongside her twins and the three others that had been born to other females of the tribe. She did not need the trees to tell her that was a good sign.

Her heart was full and the mother dogs could feel it and let Lut reach for their puppies one at a time. She lifted each of them to her nose, cooing softly as she held them.

Was there anything on earth as sweet as the smell of new life? Was there anything that made a heart swell like a soft ball of innocence? It was nature's greatest trick. Making new ones so lovable they stole your heart in seconds so you would protect them forever.

A week passed and the puppies' legs strengthened. They began to explore the world around them without falling over every other step. Lut and Ish looked their look and knew what the other was thinking.

Outside in their favorite spot, between the pine trees and the jagged rocks, the twins stopped short and came running when they heard Lut calling. Isha was not about to make that mistake again.

The twins looked at each other and broke into giggles, knowing their wait was over. Lut had waited a week even though they begged her to let them see the puppies everyday.

Lut had not been wrong. Just what she saw in her mind played out in front of her eyes. The twins ran in and their mouths opened as they saw all the puppies and felt them swarm over them, covering their faces with warm kisses.

Lut had heard happy sounds from the twins before, when she held them and swung them, tickled their arms and feet and dripped honey into their waiting mouths. But never a sound like they both made this time.

It was nothing either had learned or needed to. It needed no thought, no waiting and wondering. The shake of the small tails on the back of the pups spun them around in circles. The arms of the twins joined together to help sweep them in as the squeals jumped out of them. Ish and Lut could not hold their hahas in as the twins and the puppies rolled around and in one second all of them were one.

Lut did not let that moment pass with just laughter. What she was seeing was more than she was watching. Oohma had known another life, as the pack and the tribe all had. But the puppies would know no life without the tribe. They would know no other way to live but being with the tribe and hunting with the tribe and sleeping among them and sharing their lives and their food.

The high-pitched squeals of the twins brought Lut back to earth to a place most lose with their years. One of pure happiness and simple joy and warm pink tongues licking, smiling small faces and fluffy soft balls of fur making giggles pour out.

CHAPTER **80**

Hun's moment turned bitter in his mouth as he stood there staring at their blank faces. Had he been home he would have raced into Lut's tent and shown her what he had done and she would yip in amazement.

The females of the tribe would be shouting screams of joy. Without being told to they would race into the fields to reap armfuls of grain and climb into the trees to pick ripe fruits while meat was roasting over the fire. It would have been a feast for all to remember, given in Hun's honor. But the moment passed with just a belch and a groan.

It was one more thing the old man and the dog had ruined for him. One more thing that had been stolen from him that he would never get back.

He would never walk to the fire with every eye on him. Walk into the center of the camp to yells and shouts of triumph. And more than anything, he would not have the raw pleasure of sharing his moment with someone who understood what it meant, someone like Lut.

A gust of wind swirled around him and a harsh *no* clicked out of him. He would have his moment, just not this moment, just not this night.

He took the meat and the other fish he had buried in the salt and put them in his sack. A sweep of his arm sent the tribe running to gather up the sacks Hun had them fill with the white crystals and lift them on their backs.

Grunts jumped from them as their legs buckled under the weight but Hun pressed them to carry more. He was beyond caring. Once they had done what he needed them to do, there would be nothing else he needed of them, especially them.

When all of them returned to their crude camp, Hun sent a spark flying and in moments a fire was blazing, jumping from the twigs to the logs. Maybe when they were back it would all come to them and they would understand as they sat around the fire. How could they not?

The tribe's faces showed no questions. None of their eyes crunched tight as they came in close to the flames. Since the day of the hyena, and now as they returned from the ocean, they followed all of Hun's instructions with no hesitation and no questions.

Whatever he said, they did and whenever they did what he said, they ate. It was as simple as that. No one complained or asked why when they were chewing.

CHAPTER 81

When all their eyes were on him, he took the sack that held the meat and dumped it out on the ground for everyone to see. Pushing the crystals aside, he took the dry body of the mole and made a motion to pass it around. Everyone was to hold it, touch it and eat some, especially the females.

Hun sat back and watched each of them bite some off, then chew down and swallow. His eyes tightened as he watched them. What would they think and do when they realized they were eating old meat that was still as good as fresh meat? Hun could hardly keep his hands still as he stood there waiting to see.

He moved from his place at the fire and walked around them, his chest puffed out beneath his lion skin, waiting for a pat on his back, or a hand on his leg, or a scream of joy for what he had done. But the only sounds he heard were teeth grinding, happy grunts and a chorus of uuums.

One of the females gave him hope when she sprinkled a few crystals of salt on her meat and yelped out for the rest of the females to do the same. He watched their eyebrows lift, their eyes widen along with their smiles and their clicks as their chewing grew louder and louder.

It was what Hun had been hoping for, what he had wanted Lut to see and had wanted Lut to be part of. But the moment passed the moment the meat was swallowed. He turned for his hut and went inside it shaking his head sadly. He had more in common with the old man's dog than with any of this tribe.

Not one of them took the dried meat past their lips into their minds. Not one of them understood it was not just food but freedom he had brought them, a way to move past the day to a tomorrow and another tomorrow after that. Their minds were on their eating. That required no thought. Next weeks meat had no meaning, it was too far away.

He sat in his hut chewing it over for hours and then he spit it from his thoughts. That moment had been taken from him but it left something behind. Their weakness was his strength. When they did what he said, they had meat to eat. That was all they needed to know, that was their only care.

The next morning, before the sun rose, they heard Hun yell for them to get up. The females followed their mates outside and Hun pointed to the ashes for them and the forest for the males. There was meat to take for the long trek ahead. That left little time to sleep.

Many moons would phase from sliver to full again before they got there. Each step would be filled with unknown dangers, but Hun did not care. He would have done it alone if he had to. The time had come.

The tribe asked no questions, they did what they were told. Hun pointed to the kind of poles he needed. How many he wanted and how much of the shiny black obsidian and flint it would take to make enough points. Spears broke and were lost in every hunt and it was harder to make them on the trail.

The one toolmaker he could trust, the one he called Arl, lean, with long hair and eyes clear and bright had proved he could do it. And four hands were faster than two.

While he and Arl were busy chipping, the tribe went to the pines and slashed into their bark until the sticky sap they used for glue ran freely into their hollow stones. When they had enough sap they turned to chopping poles and soon had a pile stripped of leaves and bark.

While they were busy with their tasks, Hun turned all his attention to Arl and made him stand up and follow him. He could throw now but Hun needed him to throw better if he hoped to take the old tribe. The moment of surprise at seeing trees walk would only last so long.

Hun took Arl to a quiet place and set his feet firmly on the ground. Legs and feet were as important to throwing as an arm.

Once his feet were planted, he turned to Arl's throw and showed him how to make it better. How to find the point of balance with his hands and how to make the right release with his fingers.

Hun kept him at it, throwing over and over until he could throw with almost as much accuracy as Hun. Then Hun stopped him.

Almost as good was as far as Hun wanted to take him, so Arl could never be a threat and never be a challenge. Not to him as a hunter, not to him as a leader. And not of interest to Lut, who might be taken by his height and full mane, young trim body and pleasant open face.

It wasn't until the old crone made Hun understand with her clicks and gestures that Arl was not one of them, but born to another tribe and taken as a boy when he was the only one left alive.

That made something he had not thought of before cross his eyes. If Arl could do more than they could, and he could do more than Arl could, were there others out there who could do more than he could? That could make their trek back more dangerous and taking the old tribe back even more important?

CHAPTER 82

She woke in the night to the sounds of gasps. Her first thought was one of the twins, but the truth was just as bad. Oohma heard it too and raced inside, pacing back and forth over him.

Lut pulled Ish up to a sitting position, to clear his windpipe. Moving behind him, she pounded on his back and moved his arms up and down until finally Ish made a rumbling sound and spit up what was blocking his breathing.

When Lut saw it her chest tightened and a sharp gasp snuck out of her. A circle of green tinged with red lay on the ground and a dribble of it dripped down Ish's chin.

Once Oohma saw and scented it, his eyes turned to Lut. His gaze filled with sadness and meaning, begging for her magic. But both knew the truth. Ish had already passed the point most others never reach and his path, as all paths did, had an end.

Oohma circled the bloody spot and turned again for Lut. She turned her eyes away but not quickly enough. Oohma saw the pain in them and it stabbed into him like the auroch's horns. Dropping his head he pulled his ears in tight and let his tail fall. Lut came up to him and put her forehead on him. She could not ease it, but she shared his pain.

If only the predator attacking Ish were a lion or a cave bear, a hyena or a bison, he would have spun and bared his teeth, thrown himself at it and fought it to death. But death never fights. It wins.

Still that day had not come yet, and Oohma shook himself and tugged at Ish's hand and Ish's eyes brightened as he used Oohma's strong back to help him stand up and steady.

Oohma had sensed it long ago. The old one had a stubborn streak. Ish would not curl up and wait. Everything a male of the tribe needed to know had to be told. And if he did not tell it, who would?

Together they moved out onto the low trail and Oohma saw a flash of dinner jump across the path. The fat rabbit took it in one long hop and scurried between a narrow green yew and the mass of thin vines growing on it.

As it disappeared Oohma shot forward. The rabbit was too close to let it go by. He leaped for the opening between the tree and the vines the rabbit had jumped into.

His aim was perfect. His snout pushed the vines aside as his head hit the yew, but then he stopped short. His body was much thicker than the rabbit's and he got stuck between the yew and the vine.

He craned his head and kicked his paws, but his paws were feet off the ground, making the tangles worse. The rabbit never looked back as it escaped into the brush. But Ish could not look away as he watched Oohma's paws try to run on air.

CHAPTER 83

Ish could not help it, hahas roared out of him when he saw Oohma stuck like a fly in a spider's web. When they stopped he called to Oohma to stay still. He was coming to help. Moving as fast as he could, Ish hobbled down the rocky hill.

He knew Oohma still remembered the vines and hated them. He put a reassuring hand on his head when he got to him, and clicked softly as he pulled out his knife.

The branches were so bushy, Ish struggled to trim them back to the trunk before he could get the vines loose. His blade was sharp and in minutes, with the branches gone, just one vine was holding Oohma in.

Ish pulled, making Oohma yelp. All his struggling had wrapped the vine so tightly around his paw it was biting into his flesh. Ish could not get it loose with his gnarled, stiff hands and cutting into it with his blade could mean cutting into Oohma.

He looked around quickly for something that could help. All he could find was a stick about three feet long with a pointed tip on one end and a shape like two short fingers spread apart on the other.

Ish wedged it into the vine while he held Oohma's paw in his hand. He pushed back at it with all that he had. It loosened just enough and Oohma didn't wait another second. With another sharp yelp he pulled his paw free and slid out of the vine that held him.

With Oohma free, Ish let the stick go. His breath caught in his throat when he saw what the bent yew and the vine had done. They had sent the stick flying 80 paces or more. Oohma raced up the hill, happy to be free, and barked out at Ish to call him. But Ish wouldn't come. His legs could not move. He'd been captured.

Even when Ish was young and straight and strong, he could never throw a spear that far. No one, not even Hun could even come close. Ish dropped his hand and limped to the place the stick landed. He picked it up and carried it back as Oohma stood watching him from the top of the hill.

His hand was shaking when he stood behind it again and notched it in. His old arm quivered as he pulled the vine back, bending the yew as he did. He held his breath when he let the stick fly.

The sound of it hitting the ground made his breath rush out. Just like it did the first time, it flew out but this time farther.

Ish walked around it and aimed his blade at the yew. A few sawing motions and it was cut loose and in his hand. But the vine he left on it, attached to the top and bottom.

All that afternoon, Ish shot the stick forward, trying to see how far it would go until the inside of his arm was raw and bloody from the sting of the vine.

He'd been a hunter all his life and had killed from close in and killed from far back and he knew what all hunters knew. The farther back you kill from, the longer you stay alive.

He didn't need Oohma's help as they walked back to the camp. His steps quickened as a fresh surge of energy pulsed through him.

He stopped to gather in a few more straight sticks but changed his mind. The bushes around the camp held as many as they would need and what he needed more than sticks was Lut.

Every few steps Oohma heard a haha pop out of him as the winds blew around them. They were telling Ish that they would come for him but not yet.

They walked into camp and every eye turned to follow them. Every question on their faces was about one thing. The long yew pole with the taut vine tied to it strung across Ish's shoulder.

All knew when Ish or Lut or Oohma brought something back to the camp, it would be something to see and be told about as they sat by the fire. But Ish did not say a word. He looked at them and looked at the sky.

Lut watched him take the bow and bring it to his chest. Her forehead wrinkled when she saw him take a long stick and notch it into the thin vine. Her mouth went tight and she made no sound as Ish drew the stick back, held it for a moment, then let it fly.

No eye was anywhere but on it as it leaped from his bow, sailed through the air, then came back down long paces away.

Lut gleamed as she watched Ish's sticks fly. *The old man*, she thought, her heart filled with pride.

CHAPTER 84

She was not blind. She had seen the looks other females gave her at the thought of mating with an old man when their mates were young and strong.

But Lut had her own look when she saw their look. Every young one in the tribe, if they were put together as one, could never be Ish or do what he had done. The thought of all that was all over her every time she looked back. And when she did, all the females bent their heads down again and looked away.

Their mates were young but would one day grow old as all men do. Wither and weaken, stoop over and die. But whose man would be sung about when theirs were no longer even a memory?

Lut looked over at Ish as the tribesmen surrounded him, clicking and yelping and waiting their turn at Ish's new magic. Her eyes sparkled as the sunlight glinted off them. A week with old Ish was worth a lifetime with anyone else.

Moc, the short, stout male with the ready laugh who had brought the drum from the forest heard the sticks leave the bowstring with different ears.

It was not how far it sent them but the sound the vine made when the sticks flew out that made his skin prickle and a low whistle blow past his lips.

When the bow was passed to him, instead of fixing a stick and shooting the air, he plucked at the taut string and held it to his ear, listening to the vibrations change each time he snapped it.

When he passed on the bow, he headed into the nearby forest. Curved branches and vines wouldn't be hard to find. He blew out different sounds as he searched through the brush and the sounds of his voice climbing up and down started spinning through him. If one string sang like that, he thought as he listened to his own sounds, what could five do?

Moc was not the best hunter, that all the tribe knew, but when they listened to his sounds it did not matter. His hunt brought things to the tribe none of the others could.

Next to the meat, there was nothing he liked more than dragging in something he had found and seeing what the tribe would think. The drum he had brought them weeks before had them jumping to their feet. But this was more than the drum. What these strings could sing would drive them wild.

All that day he worked to find wood that did not sound dead when he tapped on it and had enough of a curve to fit enough vines. Finally he found one lying behind some boulders that was dry enough and light enough. He chopped it to size with his ax, then took his blade and cut some grooves into the top and bottom of the wood.

When the grooves were as deep as the vines were thick, he wrapped them as tight as they would let him without snapping. He took a deep breath and blew out his whistling sound and put his fingers on the strings.

Sounds had always moved him, but not like these did. They jumped into his ear, ran down his arm and dove into his chest, making his heart pound and his feet tap on the ground.

For hours he sat there plucking, listening to the sounds the vines made as his fingers ran up and down them. He heard what each string said when plucked one way and what it said when plucked at with a different speed and pressure.

He paced back and forth waiting for darkness so he could bring it to the fire and sit next to his brother with the drum.

CHAPTER **85**

The pile of chipped points, long straight poles and pools of pinesap grew. And the more it grew, the better they got at it. They still didn't have a throw worth throwing but their slabbing could find a target and kill. And their mud disguises would let them get close enough to slab while he and Arl did the rest.

Hun pushed them mercilessly but spun dreams for them about the place he would take them, to push them on. A better place, a richer place, one filled with all they would ever want and things they did not even know. It lay just beyond the hills where he came from. He knew the way. He would take them there and they would take it for themselves.

Taking as many spears as they could carry, he took Arl and put him right behind him and waved his arm for the rest to follow. He longed to see Ish's eye pop out of his old head as he ran down the hill into the camp. The look on Ish's face when he saw that he had not sent Hun to his death, but himself to his own. That would be a moment like no other.

He was strong when he left, but stronger now with a new tribe and new spears and the precious white crystals. They would knock the old man to the ground and knock Lut off her feet.

Hun clicked and nodded sadly at how fast the camp came down. He could see that everything they had to bring with them he had brought to them, except for the mud. Why had they stayed so long where they were when there were hills around them with deep caves and the sea beyond the hilltops that teemed with life? But with no one to lead them, who were they to follow?

No one grumbled or cursed as they kept on trudging toward the rising morning sun. Hun had been smart enough to fix the sun's position on the morning he left the old tribe and he kept moving toward it each day as it began to climb.

There were other things Hun fixed in his mind and he saw some he remembered as they moved. Trees that bent and twisted in familiar ways. Rocks that looked like bears or lions, vistas Hun knew he had seen before. The day of return was getting closer. He could already smell it in the air.

CHAPTER 86

Oohma was restless. More than once he climbed to the top of the hill and craned his neck, turning his nose in every direction. But each time he came back down, there was nothing in the air that should not be there.

It had been so long since Hun had been pushed out, the memory of him was fading. Either he was dead or lost by now or too far away to think about. But for the last few days Oohma's ears had been perking and his nose had been twitching without telling him why. Something was coming at them that wasn't there yet. He could feel it in his bones.

When Oohma padded back down from the hilltop, he saw Ish was busy pointing at the tribesmen, splitting their tasks in two.

While the males did their jobs, the females did others. They took long, subtle stands of vine and stood wide apart. Coming back together, they twirled the thin vines into strong strings that could stand up to the snap of the bow and push the sticks where they were aimed.

This new thing made Ish's hands shake with excitement. Except for one thing, the thing that stole his sleep.

The sticks left his bow flying straight but then they began to wobble, often hitting their target sideways instead of head on. Or they fluttered out and fell back to the ground in the middle of their climb.

Ish did not notice that happening when his target was the sky and his excitement came from just watching the sticks fly. Now he knew he had jumped too fast.

He walked to a flat rock and sat down hard, his head in his hands and his elbows on his knees watching each shooter's stick start out good and then go bad.

The sticks were good for 80 paces, sometimes 90, but then they lost their power and direction. Ish had planned to chip down some of the spear points and put them at the heads of the sticks. But he knew the weight of the points would make the sticks wobble even more.

A loud cawing lifted his head. The sky above him was filled with black birds drawing circles on the clouds. Something must have died below them, making them send out nature's signal for all the forest to see.

The predators would take some first but leave behind a little meat the black birds' beaks could not have reached. Then the ants would come and take their share and leave the rest for the earth to devour. All that lived in the forest lived by its rules. Everything that comes from it returns to it when the time comes.

He loved watching the birds lift off, ride the wind and tilt up and down, keeping their bodies balanced and steady. He moved his hands with them as they moved with the wind, letting it carry them, rather than fight it.

When the day birds came in for the night, the night birds flew out. Ish cupped his hand above his eye as they moved through the shadows and landed without a wobble or a fall.

Lut brought him a bowl to drink. He ate little now but Lut could see that he needed one of her brews to keep his energy up. The blood in his spit and the shake in his legs took her sleep, but gave her no answers but the simple one, the only one. There were no answers. Still she needed to do what she could do for as long as Ish needed her.

Ish took the bowl and sipped at it in spite of its taste. Still, the faraway look stayed on his face. He tried to take it apart piece by piece, as he would if he were tracking prey. Sign by sign, spore by spore.

Two things were true and that's where he would start. The sticks flew and birds flew. They both took off flying straight but the bird continued on while the sticks fluttered out. The birds did not wobble but the sticks did. What was the secret the birds had that the sticks did not know? He would watch and he would see.

He signaled for Oohma to stay back that day with Lut and the twins and not follow him out onto the trail. Oohma dropped his tail and walked back to Lut. What Ish needed to do Oohma could not be part of. Even if he did not mean to, he would scare the crows away.

As he rounded the hill and walked into the meadow, waves of black birds flew in and out of the gnarled olive trees. He found a log close by and sat watching their heads bob up and down as the olives fell. Old ones shriveled and rotted as they lay on the cool, moist dirt, bringing out the worms the birds were waiting to eat.

How easy it must be to be a black bird, Ish thought. He watched them waiting in the pale green leaves letting the tree do the work before they flew down and plucked a fat worm from the ground.

Ish watched one come in close to him, its yellow eyes watching him as closely as he watched it. Everything the bird did meant something and Ish needed to find out what.

No matter their size or shape, their color or their look, Ish saw them do the same thing. When any bird came to land they spread their tail feathers and came down without a wobble.

Every time he saw them do it the same question kept jumping out at him. What did the birds have that the sticks did not?

Bird after bird, takeoff after takeoff and landing after landing, Ish watched until he could see them in his sleep, spreading their back feathers before their feet touched down.

Animals talk if you listen. Ish had lived his life knowing that. It was the reason he still lived and he sat there all day with his ears and eye wide open. It took a thousand birds, maybe more, spreading their tail feathers for Ish to understand their secret. Finally he did. The birds had feathers at their back and his sticks did not. It took Ish one second to fly off the rock and grab a long pole.

A nest, dry and empty, was close enough to reach and Ish swung at it until he hit it. When it hit the ground Ish found a few long black feathers stuck inside it. He pulled one out and laid it on the ground.

The center of the feather split easily in half as his blade sliced through it. The pinesap that he used on the spear points worked even better on the feathers. He coated their quills and pressed half a feather onto each side of the stick.

When it felt dry and tight he stepped a good distance back from a tree, put the feathered end of the stick in the string of the bow and drew it back.

The instant he let it go he saw it spin through the air, not wobble. He saw it head straight for the spot he aimed at and saw it dig in when it hit. He screamed out a shout of thanks to the birds for showing him their secret. What once was a stick was now an arrow.

CHAPTER **87**

At the first crack of dawn Hun stood all of them together, let each eat a few bites and began pushing them forward. The path to the old tribe was merciless but he knew of no other way to get there.

Just keep the rising sun out front in the morning as it had been at his back when he left. Fix the place it climbed out of each day and walk toward it as straight as the landscape would allow.

Before they left he made each of them, female and male, even the old one, stand on a large animal skin. When he pulled out his knife the one closest to him jumped back, not sure what Hun would do.

But Hun grabbed the male's ankle and pressed his foot down on the skin. He drew his blade around it, leaving a few extra inches to work with.

When he had the shape of their feet cut out he made the sign that said, *Watch me*. Running his blade along the edges, he left slits wide enough to string a leather strap through.

Jagged stones had always cut through the thin woven sandals they had worn. It was another gift Hun had brought them. Like he had brought them meat and fire, spears and blades and now what they had on their feet. Why would they not follow his footsteps anywhere they took them?

Still, he could feel the anxiety of the tribe growing as they followed him day after day, as days became weeks and months and food grew short and their water was low. He could see their eyes dart back and forth, knowing the forest was full of predators they could not see, waiting for them to take one bad step.

And the path they were on was made of bad steps and endless challenges, raging rivers and steep canyons and violent storms that soaked them and the ground.

There was no day when a fat lazy rabbit crossed their path and hopped onto their flames. No day when a tree heavy with fruit toppled over into their laps. Just sharp drop-offs and slippery, graveled slopes and piles of rocks hiding coiled snakes and buzzing flies and biting bees.

Hun had been moments from death more than once as he fled the old tribe. And he was sure one of them or more of them would not have his luck and would come to the end of their trail.

Hate and anger had fueled his coming. They had helped him and driven him on against all reason. Given him the strength to defy all the dangers and pain he was in and the will to beat them alone.

Still. What he had now was worse than being alone and it made their trek even harder. Two young mothers with their babies slung in front so they could feed them and keep on walking and one old one who could barely walk at all. Maybe, Hun laughed to himself as he watched her being carried, they would get lucky and she would die along the way and they could go faster without her.

The winds had grown sharper day by day and the nights longer. It surprised Hun how quickly he had grown used to sleeping inside something and not outside with nothing but a skin and the fire. It made his need to get there burn even hotter inside him.

Shielding his eyes he took a long look at the sun, fixing its position again. There it was, clear as day. And the sun never lied. He had set out with it rising at his back and now he was heading back at it again. There could be no other way.

Each day as they had set out, Hun sent out a different male who could move much faster alone than with the tribe. His search was for places where they could sleep out of the weather and out of danger each night. If a cave could be found it usually had something living in it not looking for neighbors. And large rock overhangs and natural shelters were few, if any at all.

The warmer days when they began had been filled with sunshine. But the farther they walked, the more it rained. Making walking harder, sleeping miserable and fires impossible to keep lit.

How long it kept on would determine how long they could go on. But with them or without them, Hun was going back. If his spears didn't work the sacks of salt would. They had to. There could be no other way.

CHAPTER 88

Ish sat there beaming. Every time one of the tribesmen's arrows sliced through the air and found its mark, he lifted his spear and pounded it on the ground.

How far an arrow could travel and how true its path could be brought shouts of joy from his wrinkled lips. It was almost as if the feathers were still a bird, still alive, teaching the arrows to fly.

A feeling of pride poured into him with all its warmth. Every step Ish and Lut and Oohma had taken together had taken them miles ahead. Between the arrows and the dogs, the flocks and the fields, unless a fire came and ate the forest there would always be a place to sleep and food to eat.

When the best of the spear throwers could not come close to the least of the arrow shooters, even on his weak legs Ish spun and stamped his feet.

He did not stop until he could barely stand and the forest was spinning around him.

The distance a spear travels could be reached in a few long leaps. But an arrow could fly 50 times farther with much greater accuracy and move so fast that Oohma could not catch one. A lucky leap by Oohma or the pack could catch a spear in mid-air but never an arrow. He was right when he told them they knew their spears well enough. It was time to master their bows.

Nights at the fire were no longer just for eating and exhaustion but were now filled with a constant clicking and the sound of hahas flying back and forth. Tomorrows that were once looked at with fear had come to be filled with promise.

Oohma saw that, just like his, the tribe's pups were fatter and their sounds were happier and more of them survived and grew tall and straight and strong. It was as easy to read the mood of the tribe as it was to sense the mood of the pack. All was at peace, even the winds and the fire.

The pack couldn't get enough of the feelings the tribe set off inside them. They had come to need touch as much as meat and they learned to do the things that made the tribe touch them more. Laying their heads on the laps and legs of the ones they had chosen to be theirs. Wagging their tails, panting happily and some even rolling on their backs, their paws hanging on their chests.

That always brought a happy burst, especially when one of them moved their back leg when one of the tribe scratched their stomachs.

Their grins grew even wider when Moc, the music maker, came to the fire and showed his face. Everyone could see there was something bursting out of him. Something he could not wait to show them. But their brows knit tight again when they saw what Moc was holding in his hand.

Why had Moc brought his bow to the fire when theirs were leaning up against the wall? And why were there five strings on Moc's bow when there was only one on theirs?

They soon found out Moc's bow was no bow. When he lifted it, it started to sing. And when he picked at the strings and his brother joined in, picking up the beat on the drum, none of the tribe could stay sitting where they were. Even the dogs jumped around with them as they leaped around the fire.

Oohma did not understand it. His ears had heard many sounds, from shrill whistles to rumbling roars, but never ones like these. He could see that they did more than listen. They let the sounds come into their bodies and live on inside them.

When they were on their feet shaking their heads and clapping their hands, Moc began to tell a story with his song. It told of a bee that could fly through the air and not be caught when it flew out to sting.

Oohma watched the tribe take the sounds Moc made and say them back again and again as the meaning of the bee stings came to them. Some used their fingertips to be the bee, stalking and landing, aiming and sting-ing, and all knew the bow was the bee and its sting was the arrow.

Lut pulled Oohma in closer and sat him down next to the twins as her body swayed to the sounds that Moc and his brother made. The whispers had told her the sounds were like the mushrooms she had found, taking the tribe places they can't get to themselves. Bringing them sounds they've never heard before.

And Moc, his square shoulders and squat body holding up his large head, he was their mushroom taking them along with him, showing them the way.

It happened so easily, Moc didn't know how or why. He just did it. Something moved inside of him and he moved his fingers across them and sounds jumped off the strings with a voice of their own. Sounds that had meaning without words. That could touch without hands and feel without fingers.

Moc loved the tricks the strings had taught him. Some could make the heart heavy and some could make the heart feel light. Some sounds could bring sleep while others could bring a sway. That was their magic.

The moment they heard him, Ish and Lut decided that was all Moc should do. Just like Baba made pictures and did not hunt, so too the tribe would feed Moc and his drummer brother while they made their songs. They were no different than the planters and pickers in the fields or the hunters in the forests or the makers of pots and the cookers of meat. All brought the tribe things that made their life better. Some for their stomachs, some for their eyes and some that climbed into their ears and came out their feet.

CHAPTER 89

Four moons had waxed and four moons had waned before Hun saw them, the craggy outlines of a mountain peak that looked like a man looking down at the valley.

He knew it and it made his heart leap to see something he knew was from home. His weariness leaked out of him when he saw it. The others behind him had to run to keep up.

The moment he had seen that they were hunters, not trees, and how close he had to get to them to know it, he knew how he would use them. And each night, especially in the rain and mud and misery, he could see Ish's face go from shock to pain then death when a tree walked up to him and jammed a spear into his chest.

Hun would not let that moment pass without seeing Ish see his face. Without Ish knowing it was Hun who was sending him to the place beyond the clouds. He spit when he said it. The mighty Ish would not be so mighty when he left his life behind on the end of his spear.

A few more miserable nights and they'd be there. And he'd be sleeping in a warm tent with the warm skin of a woman next to him. He'd sprinkle some of the white crystals on strips of the stag that still were good after all these months. Lut would roll over on her back for him.

Once he knew by the landscape around him that they were just one day out, he would stop them and get the mud out. And all would put some on so even if they were seen by one of the old tribe they wouldn't be seen. They'd just be trees in the forest. And even if one of the old tribe saw any trees walk they would not believe their eyes, just turn and run away.

Each time Ish followed Oohma out, he had to put his hand on Oohma's head to settle him down. But Oohma would not stand still. His lip pulled back showing his snarling teeth.

He stalked to the edge of the camp and circled it, lifting his leg over and over as he went. Something strange was sneaking into the air just at the edge of his senses.

Oohma did not stay with Ish as he usually did, but raced to put the pack on high alert. He divided them up knowing their strengths. Which of them were faster, which of them were stronger, which of them was the most ferocious. Which to stay in the fields to protect the flock and which to move forward to protect the camp.

Each of the pack understood the strategy they would follow as they readied for the moment. It was part of them, letting them hunt together and coordinate an attack by how they moved. The only way that could happen was to know what the others in the pack would do. To rely on that without thinking.

Hun held his spears in his hand and tightened his hand around them as though they were living things that might jump out. The night was cold and the winds harsh but he could not start a fire. A whiff of smoke on the horizon would make the old tribe look too hard.

But the real danger was the new tribe. What would they do when the moment came? That was something Hun could not be sure of. When they came upon a tribe of real hunters who knew how to hunt and throw and attack, what would happen then?

Hun walked around their small camp, walking off the pounding in his head. Telling his shoulders to loosen. Telling his hands to stop shaking. Telling himself to sit down and wait.

He had waited this long. He had suffered this much and come this far. He could last a little longer. He had to. They needed to get their mud on and disguise themselves as trees and like it or not he'd have to wait for morning.

CHAPTER **90**

*As the sky lightened, the pack became a howl-
ing mass. Their hair bristled up and down their
backs and their heads cocked back and forth as
their noses searched the air.*

They could smell a pack with a scent like the tribes. But even with their
sharp eyes they could see nothing. Just hear leaves rustling in the forest
even though there was no wind.

The tribe rushed up and, like Oohma, they saw nothing threatening.
Nothing strange was moving anywhere. But the tribe trusted the dogs
more than they trusted themselves.

If they were warning something was coming, something was coming and
the only thing to do was get ready.

Each picked up a bow and a handful of arrows, checked their blades at their waists, kept their spears close by and stood deadly still waiting for Ish's orders.

He limped up to lead them. But to where? Where was the threat so he would know where to aim their bows? He did not know and they did not know. But Oohma did.

He trusted his nose more than his eyes. Something could look like it was when it wasn't but nothing could smell like it wasn't when it was.

Oohma swept his nose around again and there was more than one of them but a tribe of them. And one of them was a scent he knew well. A scent he hated. It was Hun.

This was the moment Oohma had searched the wind for every day and he was ready. He had watched Ish use his finger to drive Hun away, but it would not be a finger Hun would feel tearing through his throat. No warnings this time. Only blood.

Oohma turned and showed the pack his teeth to show them what he meant. He started down the hill slowly, keeping them behind him but ready.

When he reached the line he had laid down, he stopped and waited for Ish and the tribe to catch up. Ish was the leader. Oohma stood there, the pack behind him, waiting for him to throw out his arm and bark out his orders telling them to go.

They were close. Maybe 200 steps away. They stood there clicking and pointing. Ish held them back.

He saw it. But he could not believe his eye. Now he understood Oohma's reactions. The trees in front of them were not trees but tribesmen. And Hun was with them, covered like they were with leaves and twigs and mud.

Ish felt Lut trembling behind him. She never thought she would see Hun again, but there he was. Ish reached back to her. There was nothing Hun or the strangers could do.

No spears could reach that far. And they had bows and handfuls of arrows to keep them from getting any closer.

Ish had never thought it would happen, thinking he had seen the last of Hun. But now he was here and now he had some new things to show him. The taste of that was sweet, like honey on his tongue.

The bitter taste of blood and fight was pumping through Hun. He could not stay still, not for one second more. Ish took a step forward and Hun took a leap toward him closing the gap between them.

Hun was cunning. He was drawing the old man into range. No one in either tribe had ever thrown as far and hard as Hun could. But he did not know what Ish knew or what the old tribe held in their hands.

Ish's mouth bent upward as Hun's eyes tightened down. He blew out sharp noises to taunt him. Noises that Hun had loved braying at others, Ish blew back in his face.

The crimson of hate and rage bled through the browns of mud on Hun's body and made the leaves on his arms and legs shake like the wind as he struggled to control his fury.

Ish just looked at him, like he was nothing more than a dead tree in the forest. Then he puffed up his chest like Hun had done and strutted around in front of him. Oohma could hear Hun's sharp brays rip even louder when Ish turned his back to Hun and bent over.

Even from 200 steps away, Ish's taunts thundered around him, eating into to him, crossing his eyes with rage. He had waited for this moment and he could not wait one second more.

333

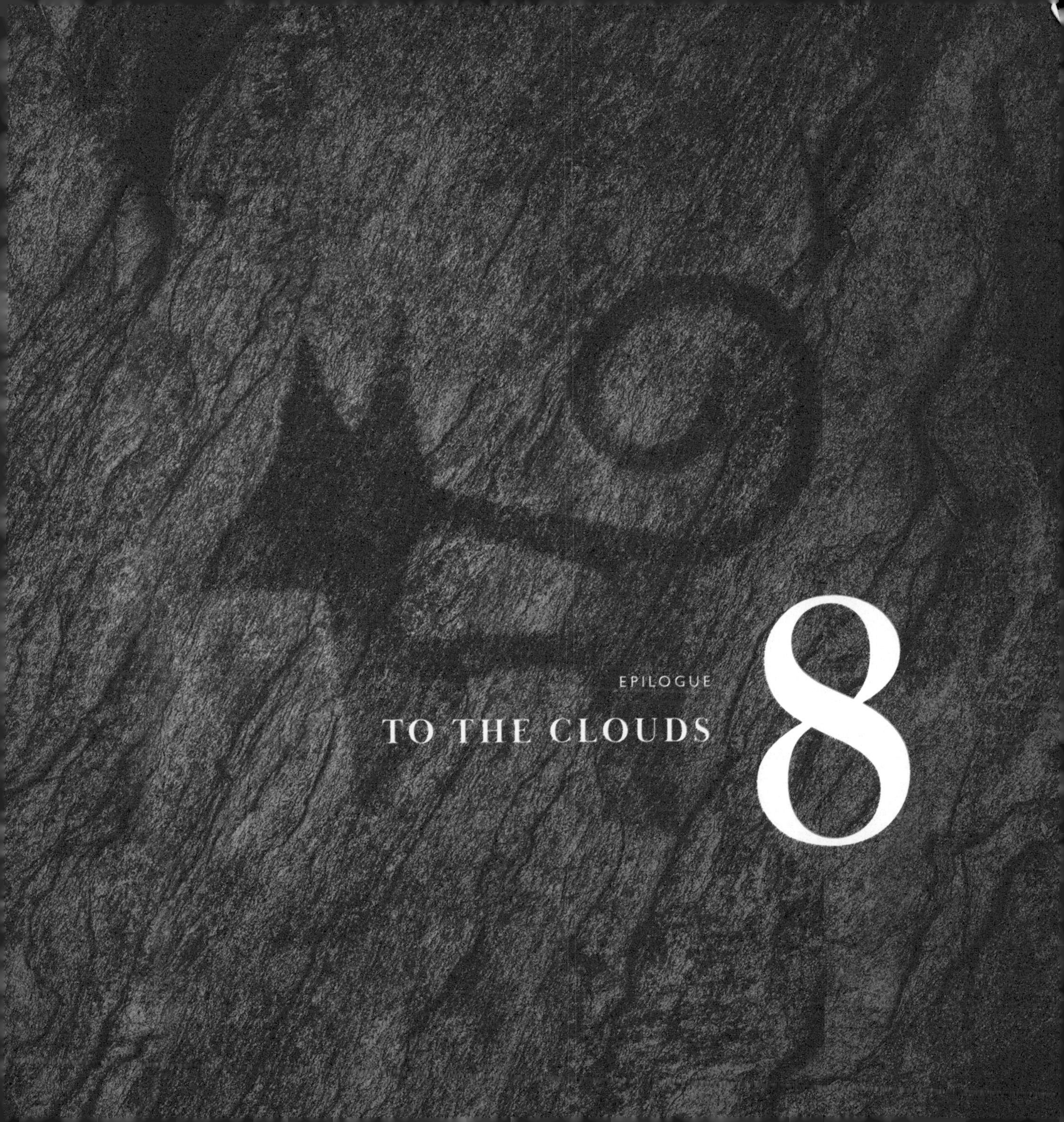

EPILOGUE

8 TO THE CLOUDS

CHAPTER 91

Hun's hand shook as he drew back his branch-covered arm. With more strength than even he knew he had, he threw his spear straight for Ish's chest. Ish saw it coming but did not move. He knew he was beyond Hun's range and Hun's spear could never reach him. That all the tribe knew well. But Oohma did not know that.

All he knew was that a spear was coming at Ish and Oohma could not let that happen. He burst out with explosive speed, his paws pounding the hard ground as he raced it down. Nothing would take Ish and nothing would harm him. Not while he was near.

It was only six inches from him but that was six inches too far. And he was six inches too fast. Putting him six inches in front of where he should have been. Instead of catching it in his mouth, Hun's spear caught him in his neck.

For a moment nothing moved, not the air or the tribes or the birds in the trees. Then Ish shot his bow and the tribesmen followed and every arrow found its mark.

They stabbed into the tree and the tree could not shake them out. Only a drizzle of white crystals spilled from Hun's sack as he fell over and choked on his last sound.

Hun opened his eyes with the last of his strength, just wide enough to see Ish's face watching him die. The death he had planned for Ish. As his last breath wheezed out of him the truth rushed in. All he had ever wanted, all he had ever dreamed of, he had once had and it wasn't Ish and Oohma who had taken it from him, but himself.

The barking and howling were deafening, but the tribe was deadly still. Lut broke the silence first and fell to her knees. A wail of pain and heartbreak broke out of her as she saw Oohma's lifeless body, pierced by Hun's bloody spear. And Hun a dead tree on the ground with arrows sticking out of him.

Seeing Hun lying still, they knew he was dead. After the first of them did it the rest of the tree tribe did it. They dropped their spears on the ground and fell on their knees, their arms above their heads holding up their sacks of white crystals as a plea to take them in and an offering of peace.

No one moved as Ish screamed seeing Oohma not moving and Lut at his side kneeling and weeping. A pain stabbed into him crushing the breath out of his chest and shot down his arm.

With the last of his strength, just the strength of his will, Ish came and stood with Lut, seeing through his tears what she saw through hers. And then he looked down at the tree lying there.

A hot anger fired inside him twisting his face. Even though there were arrows sticking out of him, some driven in to their feathers and out his back, Ish grabbed a spear and jammed it into Hun's dead body. Again and again until he could no longer breathe. Until bloody pieces of Hun's body were scattered everywhere on the dirt. Then he turned back to Oohma.

It was the longest distance he had ever traveled in his life. The few inches between Oohma being alive and Oohma being dead. Between a life that he had grown to love and the companion that had come out of the forest and into his life.

His knees buckled and he sank down next to him. Taking Oohma's head in his trembling hands he chanted the death song of a warrior in a voice that was barely a squeak. When the chant ended Ish bent his head down and put it on Oohma's torn body and began to weep.

Lut swept her arm around making all of them leave so Ish could be left with Oohma and his grief. Only she stayed behind. But she turned her back and moved to the edge of the hill so Ish could be alone to say what he alone had to say with no one but Oohma to hear it.

When she thought enough time had passed, she went over and took Ish's shaggy head in her hands and hummed his favorite sound. He put up no fight.

She rubbed his head and then his face and waited for him to open his eye. But it did not open. She said his name louder and louder but his ears no longer heard. Rolling him over Lut put her hand on his heart and she could feel it. It was broken just like hers.

CHAPTER **92**

Lut had known the moment would come one way or another. Still she stood above Ish's lifeless body too stunned to cry or move or think.

The tribe all watched her knowing there were no words or deeds to bring life back, even for the medicine woman and all she knew.

Finally, her face sagging and her lip quivering, she turned to face another moment just as bad. Telling Lutta and Isha that Oohma and Ish were dead.

She held them tight until their tears ended. The tribesmen fell to their knees and scooped out a hole deep in the earth, wide enough for two, as Lut had told them to do.

They lowered Ish in first and then put Oohma at his side and covered them both with praise and dirt and flowers. Isha stepped up first and bowed his head and took the spear Ish had made for him and put it in the grave and waved his little hand goodbye. Lutta came next and took some bones for Oohma and Ish's favorite fruits and put them there to feed them on their travels.

When their moment ended Baba stepped up and lowered a large flat slab of wood, placing it carefully next to Lutta's and Isha's tributes. On it he had repainted his most treasured memory. Ish and Oohma racing together at the wind, with nothing between them but love.

Before the rocks were piled on, Moc took a slender, grainy bone to his lips. Days before he had carved holes in it to suck out the marrow. When he blew back in, a note floated out and touched the air, then touched it again as he moved his fingers across the holes. He leaned his head back and breathed Ish and Oohma on their way.

As the flute's final notes faded out, Lut and the twins stepped away and let the tribesmen pile their grave high with stones so all would know where their heroes lay and none could disturb their journey.

At the fire that night, once eyes were dry, songs were sung and tales were told of Ish and Oohma as there would always be, as long as there were fires and dogs and tribes huddled around them together.

Moc pulled the strings and his brother beat the drum but the sounds that night were different. Low and slow and somber that kept their bodies still.

The pack and the puppies lay close to the tribe and the heat of the fire and even in the pain of loss all of them shared the same warm feeling. Ish and Oohma were together now. Forever in the place beyond the clouds.

And now that they had found each other, dogs and tribes would be together forever, sharing their tents, sharing the fire, sharing the hunt and the meat and sharing their lives together.

Lut put her hands on the twin's heads as they held the puppies each had chosen to be their own. A smile cut through her tears as her memories of Ish eased their loss.

The day would come when they all would be together again. But not yet, there was still so much more to be done. So much more that would make Ish and Oohma's spirit reach them, even from the clouds.

THE END

AFTERWORD

In 1914 in Oberkassel, Germany, researchers uncovered a ceremonial gravesite holding the bones of humans and their dogs buried together side by side.

Though the bones were ancient, the story of the extraordinary love affair between humans and dogs keeps being told. It's one that reaches from the dawn of humanity out into the infinite future.

Those first dogs that consciously came out of the forest and chose us as their companions have now grown to more than 900 million, many still in the wild and 340 recognized breeds from a Chihuahua to an English Bull Mastiff.

But no matter their size or their shape, every dog shares one innate thing. Their love for us.

Whether that first dog was Oohma or some other, long forgotten by memory and time, its legacy lives on as we come to understand on the deepest level that one of the greatest gifts ever given to mankind was the dog.

They just might be the reason that back in a cold distant past we first learned the warmth of that love.

ABOUT THE AUTHOR

Irv Weinberg is an internationally known marketing and advertising executive turned novelist with more than 30 years' experience leading accounts for major brands. During his long Madison Avenue career, he led creative teams at the world's premier advertising agencies, including Y&R, Lintas USA and Grey.

Irv is best known for creating *The Magic of Macy's*; *For the Seafood Lover in You* (Red Lobster); *America's Most Misunderstood Soft Drink* (Dr. Pepper); *Just for the Taste of It* (Diet Coke); and similarly iconic ad campaigns for British Airways, Continental Airlines and many more from start-ups to Fortune 100 companies.

Along the way he won every major award in the advertising industry, notably the Gold Lion at Venice, The One Show in New York and the Best 100 Commercials of all time, to name but three. His Dr. Pepper campaign is in the permanent collection of the Advertising Hall of Fame.

As an entrepreneur, Irv co-founded Poochi, the world's first pet fashion company and the force behind America's "dress your pet" craze, now a global phenomenon.

His novel *First Dog on Earth* is the story of the first wolf to cross over, leave its pack behind and join the family of man.

Irv currently lives in Puerto Vallarta, Mexico. He has three kids, two dogs and one mission: to create stories that make you say wow. You can follow his ex-pat adventures if you Google *Blue-Eyed Boy in Mexico*, his travel and philosophy blog of self-discovery.

ACKNOWLEDGEMENTS

Oohma was the First Dog, but it took a pack of talented humans to make him a book. It began as a conversation with a dog lover friend who told me, "Dogs domesticated themselves. We didn't bring them in. They did it consciously, on their own." And a clap of thunder hit me: One of them had to be first.

Hours of research and Werner Herzog's entrancing documentary *The Cave Of Forgotten Dreams* let me visualize my story. The fact that an early dog and a primitive boy's footsteps were fossilized on the floor of the Chauvet Cave marked the first proof of our relationship. There was my boy. There was my dog. There was my story.

First Dog on Earth became an obsession. For long moons it was my mistress, my lover, my shrink and my best friend. I poured my heart into it every single day. When it tugged my soul, I thought it would do the same to yours.

So much more than writing goes into creating a book and many co-creators deserve my thanks and respect.

Suzanne Leonard is the publisher writers dream of. A combo of smart thinking, strategic genius, shrewd insight and obviously great taste in authors.

Renowned audiobook producer David Wolf — I swear that's his last name — he and his company Audivita Studios and good karma and years of deep friendship brought me to Suzanne and her visionary company Sagacity Publishing Group.

Thanks to my close collaboration and spirited jousts with editorial director Laura Blum and director of editorial strategy Kristin Andress, my book has survived and thrived from their nips and tucks and solid thinking. They labored with love to make it the best it could be.

Kimberly Gorsuch showed me the art of the word. Her company Weeva Inc.'s exquisite design brought the book to life so it's as much a pleasure to hold in your hand as I hope you will find in reading it. Special thanks also go to Jay Spang of Audivita Studios, Cassidy Reynolds at Weeva, and Lory Moore of Sagacity Publishing Group: Their artistic flourishes illuminate the *First Dog* universe, from the website to the ebook to the print editions. Once again the greatest lesson is how much more than words it takes to make a book a book.

To my amigo Steve Wedeen who created the stunning cover, Oohma and I say WOOF!

Last but not least, my gratitude goes out to my friends, family and colleagues who generously gave their insights and love along my writing journey. There are too many to list who lent me their ears and their shoulders and now fill me with love and support.

So glad it is done. So sad it is done. Been the most invigorating challenge of my life and there have been lessons learned. The flowers on my terrace whispered to me like they did to Lut. Sometimes the last bloom of summer is the most beautiful and most precious.

YOU CAN MAKE A BIG DIFFERENCE!

Did you fall in love with Oohma the way thousands of other readers have? Reviews are the most powerful way to lead future readers to Oohma's exciting, wholesome, magical story.

Writing down Oohma, Ish and Lut's story was one of the honors and highlights of my life. Reading the thoughts, perspectives, feedback and support from my committed and loyal readers has been the icing on the cake.

If you've enjoyed *First Dog* I would be very grateful if you could spend just five minutes leaving a review wherever you purchased it. (It can be as short as you like).

Delivering this story to the world has been my labor of love. Your reviews are the fuel for the fire that spreads the love story.

Oohma and I thank you from the bottom of our hearts and paws.

Irv Weinberg

Hungry for More?

You can further explore behind the scenes and beyond *First Dog On Earth, Where It All Began,* by signing up for Oohma's tribe at https://FirstDogBook.com/fanclub.

Beyond the book, nothing gives me greater joy than giving back to my readers with extra morsels of *First Dog* goodness, including digital artwork, author interviews, editor's cuts, intriguing prehistoric facts and trivia, and other goodies exclusive only to my inner circle.

Join the club here, https://FirstDogBook.com/fanclub, and I'll send over your treats right away!

Book Club Resources

Without a doubt the most common response I get from my readers is the thirst for more, more, more of all things Oohma…so I've created a Book Club Toolkit for *First Dog* readers who want to dive deeper into "How It All Began." To download your free copy, which includes discussion questions, trivia, and even prehistoric recipes from Lut, visit https://FirstDogBook.com/bookclub.

(Of course, every thriving book club needs a passionate leader, so let us know if you'd like to be one of the special humans who guides the discussions in your part of the world!)

Give the Gift of Oohma

As much as you've enjoyed the e-book, you haven't enjoyed the full, multi sensory experience of *First Dog On Earth* until you've held a physical copy in hand, and immersed yourself in the riveting sounds of the audio version.

The gorgeous, 8"x8" bound book is an heirloom quality, illustrated masterpiece that will become a classic in your family library. The evocative audiobook was recorded in the voice of renowned voice-over actor Steve Corona, whose evocative storytelling adds unique depth and power to Irv's written word.

If you're looking to share Oohma and the tribe with others, "leave no version unturned" and gift these physical, audio and digital books to everyone on your list! This is a story every dog lover, every adventure lover, every love lover and every book lover wants to know…how it all began!

All versions available at the best price direct from my author's website at:
https://FirstDogBook.com/purchase